What readers are saying about Diary of a Real Payne

"I highly recommend this series to young [readers]. . .who also love Clementine, Judy Moody, and Ramona Quimby."
-Renee @ *Mother Daughter Book Reviews*

"My 10-year-old daughter devoured this book! Great reading material is hard to find so don't miss these fun books!"
-Renita Bentz, *Mom of Many* blog

"I cannot wait to introduce my kids to this positively authentic children's fiction title."
-Kim Teamer

"Author Annie Tipton does such a great job of allowing the reader to really invest in the characters and keep the story moving forward in a perfect pace. I highly recommend this read for ages 6 to 96!"
-A. Brooks

diary of a REAL PAYNE

OH BABY!

Annie Tipton

BARBOUR BOOKS
An Imprint of Barbour Publishing, Inc.

Print ISBN 978-1-62836-864-2

eBook Editions:
Adobe Digital Edition (.epub) 978-1-63058-576-1
Kindle and MobiPocket Edition (.prc) 978-1-63058-577-8

Cover illustration and design: Luke Flowers Creative

Published by Barbour Books, an imprint of Barbour Publishing, Inc., P.O. Box 719, Uhrichsville, Ohio 44683, www.barbourbooks.com

Our mission is to publish and distribute inspirational products offering exceptional value and biblical encouragement to the masses.

Member of the
Evangelical Christian
Publishers Association

Printed in the United States of America.
04701 0814 DP

To Nate, my kid brother.
For the first twenty years (or so),
you were my very own *Space Invader*.
But now I am so thankful to call you *friend*.

Dear Diary,

The past few months have been super busy in the Payne house. Mom, Dad, my little brother, Isaac, my dog, Bert, and I are no longer a family a five—we're a family of six! (Well, maybe five and a half.) There's a chubby, sweet, drooly, screaming, giggling, stinky, smiley, adorable reason why. Her name is Faith. She is my adopted baby sister who came to live with us soon after I got home from a week at church camp last summer. And she is crazy. And by crazy, I mean loony. Bonkers. Nutty. Cuckoo. Kooky. Insane-o in the brain-o. (You pick your favorite description.)

You might think it's not very nice of me to call a seven-month-old baby crazy, but it's one reason why I love her. Here are three more. . . .

Fun Facts about Faith:

1. *Faith's hair has a mind of its own.* Seriously, Diary, you know how I describe my hair as "basically a tragedy"? Well, Faith's is a complete tragedy. When she first came to us, she was just a few weeks old, and her mass of short, dark hair was a perfect

baby mohawk. But baby hair grows, right? Except when it falls out. And that's what Faith's hair did. One day I picked her up after a nap, and there was a clump of mohawk left on the crib mattress where her tiny head had been lying. I panicked when I saw her big ol' bald spot and had flashbacks to when I (accidentally) cut a bald spot on my brother's head. I even thought I might be able to glue Faith's hair back on. But Mom came into the nursery while I was in midplan, and she assured me that it was normal for babies to lose their first hair—and that new, permanent hair would come in. Turns out, Mom was right. Except Faith's new hair might be even more tragic than the baby mohawk. The color is still pretty and dark, but the stuff will *not* lie down. It seems poor little Faith is doomed to have spiked hair that sticks out in every direction. Mom says she will be blessed with hair that's full of bounce and body when it grows out—like the hair of a model in a shampoo commercial—but I'll believe it when I see it.

2. *Faith is a flower child.* When I found out I was getting a little sister, I had dreams of Faith following in my Converse sneaker-wearing footsteps. (I mean, how cute would itty-bitty ALL-Stars be with their little

laces and canvassy goodness?) I hoped she would choose stars to be her signature shape and maybe even red as her favorite color—to be just like me, her cool big sis, EJ. But at the ripe old age of six months, Faith had already made up her mind: she wanted flower power. Faith likes big, loopy, multicolored flowers (Mom calls them "hippy flowers") that are perfect on nursery walls, baby onesies, and wide headbands that help cover up her tragic hair. In fact, the one time I tried to dress her in adorable red corduroy overalls with a silver star on the front pocket, she screamed and screamed until I changed her clothes to a flower jumper. I tried not to take it personally.

3. Faith has two superpowers that begin with the letter S: screaming and stinking. First, the super screams. The word *loud* doesn't even begin to describe what her lungs are capable of. *Shrill* might be a better way to explain the sounds her lungs can produce, but even *shrill* doesn't quite explain it. Dad said he didn't realize the human ear was even able to hear such a high-pitched sound. For the first couple of weeks after Faith arrived, Bert took a "if you can't beat her, join her" approach to Faith's cries by howling along with her. But that got him put in his kennel in the laundry room real quick ("We don't need *two* family members

wailing," Mom said), so Bert quickly learned to retreat to his dog bed in my room and bury his head in his favorite blanket. Second, the super stink. I pride myself in having a pretty strong stomach. I've always been able to take out the trash, clean up after Bert's messes, and do other gross and smelly chores without too much trouble. But it is the absolute truth when I tell you that Faith is able to produce a smell that could cripple the evilest of bad guys. Her dirty diapers are my kryptonite! Mom says I have to learn how to change a dirty diaper without gagging before I can babysit, and I'm not sure I'll ever get there! I've tried pinching my nose with a clothespin, but somehow I can still smell it!

Faith started crawling on Christmas Day, and it's added a whole new layer of chaos to the house. If something is within her reach, she's going to find it. And immediately put it in her mouth. I actually caught her gnawing on the corner of my paperback copy of *Prince Caspian*—which, I admit, I accidentally left on the floor next to the couch. I'm not sure how long she'd been chewing on it when I snatched the book back from her, but I can tell you that it was good and drool-soaked, and now the top corners of all the pages are stuck together. It's a good thing she only has three teeth, because if she had a whole mouth full of chompers, I think she would've actually *eaten* the entire Narnia story, which would give a whole new meaning to "devouring" a good book. (I know, I know, I'm sorry—that's a corny joke only worthy of Isaac corniness.)

I feel sort of bad for Isaac because Faith's definitely stealing a bit of his spotlight. And she doesn't seem to think he's as funny as the rest of the world, either. At breakfast a couple of weeks ago, Faith was sitting in her high chair, shoving fistfuls of Cheerios into her mouth, and Isaac must've thought she looked like a captive audience for his favorite joke. You know the one, Diary. . . .

Isaac: [waves a plastic T-Rex toy in front of Faith's face to get her attention] Faith. Hey, Faithy-kins. Over here!

Faith: [closes her eyes and continues to eat Cheerios, obviously ignoring Isaac]

Isaac: Hey! Baby! [scoops up the Cheerios from the high chair tray and holds them out of Faith's reach] Listen to me!

Me: Uh, Isaac, I don't think that's a good id—

Faith: SCREEEEEEEEEEEEEEECH!

Isaac: [yells over the terrible noises coming out of Faith's mouth] Knock-knock!

Faith: AIEEEEEEEYAHHHHH!

Isaac: Faith! You're supposed to say "who's there?"

Me: [covers my ears with my hands] Isaac, she doesn't understand. Give her the Cheerios, or she won't stop screaming!

[Isaac drops the cereal on the high chair tray, and a few of them bounce onto the floor. The screaming stops as Faith's chubby fist jams Cheerios in her face like she hasn't eaten in weeks.]

Isaac: Knock-knock.

Isaac: [speaks in a high-pitched voice, pretending to be Faith] Who's there?

Me: Oh, brother.

Isaac: [back to his own voice] Noah.

Isaac-as-Faith: Noah who?

Isaac: Noah good joke?

Isaac-as-Faith: Hahaha! Oh, Isaac, you are hilarious! Good one! Hahaha!

The Real Faith: [blows soggy, Cheerio'ed raspberries at Isaac]

Isaac: Ew, Faith! [gags] A slimy Cheerio flew in my mouth! You are disgusting!

It seems to me that Isaac's just getting what he deserves. *Finally* he has a little sibling to annoy him like he annoys me. It's kind of perfect, actually.

Otherwise, Diary, things are generally great. For Christmas this year, Mom and Dad surprised me with a ukulele (with a star-shaped hole under the strings!). It's pretty much the best instrument ever, and I'm going to start taking lessons soon. One of the reasons I was so surprised to get the uke for Christmas was because the truth is that my music track record isn't stellar. I took piano lessons when I was seven, but my teacher, Mrs. Preston, gave up teaching just six months after I started. (I've always assumed she quit because I was really bad, which is kind of embarrassing, but if I'm going to be bad at something, I should at least be the worst ever.) Mrs. Preston told me it was unfortunate I didn't "have an ear" for the piano (which I assume means that I really stunk at playing), but reality check, Diary: there are eighty-eight keys on a piano, and I only have ten fingers. The ukulele only has four strings, so that means I've got six fingers to spare. I like those odds much better.

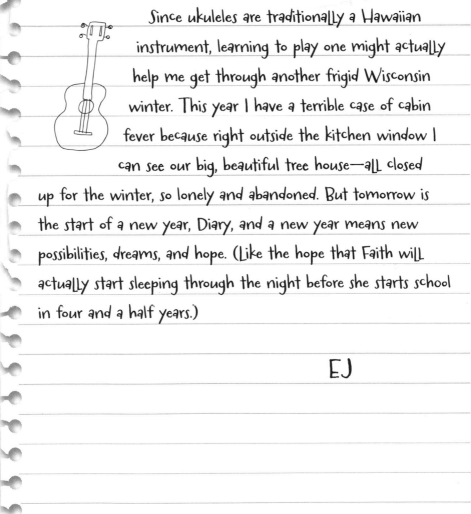

Since ukuleles are traditionally a Hawaiian instrument, learning to play one might actually help me get through another frigid Wisconsin winter. This year I have a terrible case of cabin fever because right outside the kitchen window I can see our big, beautiful tree house—all closed up for the winter, so lonely and abandoned. But tomorrow is the start of a new year, Diary, and a new year means new possibilities, dreams, and hope. (Like the hope that Faith will actually start sleeping through the night before she starts school in four and a half years.)

EJ

Chapter 1

THE DINNER DARE

Dear Diary,

The rhinovirus has invaded the Payne house.

You'd think that a fascinating word like *rhinovirus* would mean something great, like getting a new pet rhinoceros. But it's not at all great. In fact, it's sneezy and snotty and coughy and throat-hurty and generally terrible. The rhinovirus is what causes the common cold—and all five of us human Paynes have rhinoviruses stampeding through our bloodstreams.

I've been blowing my nose so much that my nostrils got red and raw. So Mom started putting Vaseline on the red part, which made it feel better until I forgot it was there and wiped my nose with the back of my hand while I was sitting on the couch watching *Mary Poppins* and trying not to think about how much my throat hurt.

Right now I can hear Dad in his study, practicing his sermon for tomorrow, except every couple of minutes or so he stops to sneeze (fun fact: Dad is a marathon sneezer, and his current record is seven in a row). Isaac is next door in time-out in his room, practicing covering his mouth when he coughs (why this is such a hard thing for him to learn, I don't know).

Mom is in the nursery with Faith, trying to squeak out a lullaby from her scratchy throat to get Faith to fall asleep for her afternoon nap.

One weird thing I've learned about babies is that they can't blow their noses. Or at least Faith hasn't mastered that skill yet. And what's even more disturbing is the fact that she doesn't seem to care if green snot streams down her face or erupts out of her nose in giant bubbles. (I wish I were making that last part up, Diary, but I'm not. She even grossed out the king of nasty, Isaac, with a snot bubble the size of a softball.) So instead of blowing her nose, Mom uses this entirely crazy thing called a nasal aspirator that sort of looks like a mini version of a turkey baster—you know, one of those things that has a plastic ball on the end that you squeeze to pick up turkey broth to squirt on the bird while it cooks? Except a nasal aspirator is like a baby baster. And instead of broth, Mom uses it to get snot and boogies out of Faith's nose.

Diary, I literally do not have the right words to explain how disgusting the nasal aspirator is.

But as disgusting as Faith generally is, she's otherwise turning out to be a pretty fun kid. There's nothing better than hearing her sweet little giggle and seeing pure joy in her eyes as she claps for fun. And now she's trying new foods all the time, and she makes some of the very funniest faces I've ever seen in my life.

EJ

"Everybody have their hands washed?" Mom set a stack of paper napkins on the kitchen table. "We've almost gotten rid of this cold bug, so let's not reinfect ourselves."

As if on cue, Dad sneezed into his elbow as he walked into the kitchen for the evening meal.

"My hands are washed *and* sanitized," EJ said, squirting a handful of bubblegum-scented hand sanitizer and rubbing both hands together furiously. EJ grinned as Faith's chubby fingers reached toward the pocket-size bottle of pink gel on the table, but it was just an inch too far from her seat in the high chair. EJ slipped the bottle in her pocket and handed Faith a set of toy car keys instead.

"Excellent job, EJ." Mom smiled at her oldest daughter and took her seat next to the high chair. "How about you, buddy? Hands washed?"

"Yep. I washed mine when I took a bath last night," Isaac said, tucking a paper napkin in his T-shirt collar like a bib. "So I'm good."

"Gross! Isaac!" EJ scrunched her nose in disgust. "I know for a fact you've gone to the bathroom since then—and you didn't wash your hands afterward?"

"Umm, I don't know." Isaac scratched his head and appeared to think hard. "Ever since I turned six, my memory is bad."

"Boys are basically a walking science experiment for germs," Dad said as he picked up Isaac and slung him over his shoulder like a sack of potatoes. "Let's exterminate our man cooties at the kitchen sink."

EJ leaned toward Faith and whispered, "Did you hear that? I *told* you boys have cooties! Dad just confirmed it!"

Faith squealed excitedly and threw the toy keys into a bowl of spaghetti sauce on the table in front of her.

Mom gingerly picked out the keys and wiped them clean with a napkin. "I guess if we're all sharing germs, at least they're *Payne* germs."

"Oh yeah, Payne germs!" Isaac said as he ran from the sink to his seat at the table. "The very best kind!"

"EJ, would you please say the prayer for our meal?" Dad took his seat at the table.

"Dear God, thank You for things like cold medicine and Kleenex and hot chicken soup and moms and dads who take care of us and help us feel better when we're sick. Thank You for always taking care of us. And thank You for this delicious"—EJ squinted to peek through her closed eyelids at the food on the table—"or at least nutritious meal that Mom made. Amen."

"Amen," Mom echoed. "Wait a second. EJ, you don't think dinner will be delicious?" She looked shocked that her daughter could say such a thing, but EJ saw the twinkle in Mom's eyes and knew she was mostly joking.

Faith had started eating solid food when she turned six months old, and Mom decided that was the perfect time to "broaden the Payne family's food palate." Which, to EJ and Isaac, meant that they would be forced to try a lot of new (mostly disgusting) foods. The only thing that made trying new kinds of food not completely terrible was that Faith made the funniest, most ridiculous faces with almost every new food that she tried.

"It *might* be delicious," EJ conceded. "But I'll let you know after dinner is over."

Along with the spaghetti sauce (delicious, according to EJ), on the table was a basket of toasted whole wheat bread with garlic butter (EJ wasn't sure about the whole wheat part of this—what happened to the Texas toast that she loved so much?); salad (a necessary evil—Mom liked to have something green on the table at every meal); and a giant bowl of what looked like spaghetti. Except vegetabley. And not at all like the pasta noodles she was used to. EJ was very suspicious that Mom was trying to pull a fast one on them.

"Marmalade, what is *that*?" Isaac used his babyish nickname for Mom and pointed at the plant-spaghetti hybrid. "It looks *weeeeeird*."

"Oh, it's super weird and fascinating," Mom said, using a pair of tongs to put a good-sized pile of the mystery food on Isaac's plate. "It's called spaghetti squash. I have no idea why God made the inside of that vegetable look like spaghetti, but at least we get to eat marinara sauce on top of it!"

Isaac held up a strand and let it dangle like a worm between his thumb and pointer finger. "Squish? Never heard of it."

"Not squish. *Squash*," EJ said. "Mom, I don't think I'll like it. May I please make a peanut butter sandwich instead?"

Isaac sniffed his piece of squash and made a face before tossing it to Bert, who sat on the floor next to Isaac's chair—prime position for a few table scraps. EJ watched as Bert licked the spaghetti squash off the floor and promptly spit it out. That was a bad sign. Bert would eat pretty much anything.

"I second the request for peanut butter." Dad looked uneasily at the bowl of yellow strands. "I'm not sure I can stomach that stuff."

EJ looked hopefully from Dad to Mom. Was she going to be off the hook for trying this new food *that* easily?

"No peanut butter." Mom's voice was firm. "Come on, you

guys, this is our chance to discover new foods. It's a good thing to get us out of our rut of mac 'n' cheese and hot dogs!"

It was true that Dad was a rather picky eater—especially for an adult—and EJ and Isaac both had inherited some of his pickiness. A couple of years ago Mom had mostly given up trying to get her family to eat things they just didn't like.

"Faith is trying new things"—Mom read off the jar of the bright purple baby food she was spooning up for Faith, who was waiting impatiently with her mouth wide open, reaching toward the food—"like this apple-blueberry-pomegranate-Brussels sprouts baby food. Wait—Brussels sprouts?"

EJ checked the label. "Yep. Brussels sprouts. Sick!"

"Okay, well, if Faith can try new food, I think we should all try it with her." Mom stuck a spoonful of bright purple baby food puree in Faith's open mouth. The family watched as Faith's lips closed around the purple stuff and waited the split second it always took her to make her very best face.

First she closed her eyes tight and flared her nostrils. Then she puckered her lips into a tiny circle. Then her eyelids opened so quickly that it looked like her eyes were going to bug out of her head. She smacked her lips in what almost sounded like a kiss, and then her tiny tongue jutted out of her mouth, pushing about half of the purple stuff onto her chin before gagging and looking a little confused at the four sets of eyes staring at her.

"She's gonna blow chunks!" Isaac shouted, ducking under the table.

Everyone laughed. The apple-blueberry-pomegranate-Brussels sprouts face was *almost* as good as the sweet potato-banana-mango-kiwi face from a few nights ago.

"See, Mom? Faith is picky just like us!" EJ said.

"Well, she *is* a Payne," Dad added.

"No, wait!" Mom said. "Look—she likes it!"

They turned their attention back to the smallest Payne, who had swallowed the remainder of the apple-blueberry-pomegranate-Brussels sprouts spoonful. Her legs kicked excitedly beneath the tray, and she opened her mouth, pleading with eyes that seemed to say, "Feed me!" With the baby spoon, Mom scraped the purple off Faith's chin and stuffed it in her mouth. While Faith's eating technique was anything but well-mannered, she actually seemed to enjoy what Mom was putting in her mouth once she got the hang of swallowing the new texture.

Dad added squash to EJ's, Mom's, and his own plate before adding a tiny pile on Faith's high chair tray, saying, "All right, everyone, if we're going to do this, let's at least make it interesting. I dare you to eat this spaghetti squash, EJ."

EJ's eyes widened. If there was one thing she couldn't turn down, it was a dare.

"I double-dog dare you to eat that spaghetti squash, Dad."

Dad narrowed his eyes at her for a second and then winked at EJ. "I triple-dog dare you!"

A triple-dog dare. That sealed the deal.

"On this episode of Dinner Dare," Mom said in her best TV-announcer voice, "we'll find out if the Picky Paynes will live up to their name or if they'll silence the skeptics and just *try* something new."

Dad threw his hands in the air. "Tabby, I was the one who *started* the dare!" EJ wasn't sure if Dad was just kidding or if he was seriously trying to get out of trying the spaghetti squash.

"And I'm the one who is *quadruple-dog daring* all three of you Picky Paynes to try it," Mom said. EJ, Dad, and Isaac looked at each other, realizing they no longer had a choice about whether they'd be trying the spaghetti squash.

"Look—Faith likes it!" Mom pointed at the baby who was chowing down on a fistful of squash. EJ's stomach lurched as she thought again how the color and texture reminded her of worms. . . .

"Welcome to Dinner Dare—everyone's favorite supper time reality contest!"

The studio audience bursts into a round of applause, nearly drowning out the game show's theme music. Colored lights swirl around EJ and the other contestants.

"Tonight's episode of Dinner Dare is sponsored by the Road Kill Café," the announcer named Tabby says. "Where their motto is: 'Today's bump on the road is tonight's delicious meal!' "

"Ewwww!" the audience chimes in together.

"We've got a great contest lined up for you tonight, folks," Announcer Tabby continues. "Please welcome the three challengers: David, Isaac, and EJ!"

A spotlight swivels to reveal the contestants, and they wave at the crowd during some polite applause.

". . .And the person you're really here to see—youngest contestant ever and reigning Dinner Dare champion: Faith!"

The crowd goes absolutely nuts—screaming, cheering, whistling, clapping, stomping—as the spotlight swoops over to reveal Faith, a sixteen-pound package of adorable chubs and crazy hair. . . .

"A baby?" EJ's eyes get wide. "A little baby is who we're going up against?"

"We can't lose to a baby, guys!" Isaac says.

"This should be a piece of cake," David responds.

"Maybe not a piece of cake," Announcer Tabby says, uncovering the table settings in front of each contestant. "More like a bowl of mealworms!"

A dinner bell clangs loudly in the background.

Faith dives into the bowl and starts devouring the worms like they're the best thing she's ever eaten.

EJ glances down at her bowl and sees the worms squirming against each other. Her stomach does a similar squirm.

"Come on, EJ, you can do this," EJ whispers to herself. "You can't let a baby beat you! You can do it!"

EJ grabs a handful of mealworms, squeezes her eyelids closed, and pinches her nose shut. Before she can change her mind, she rams the worms into her mouth and swallows them whole.

"Whoa. Hard core, EJ," Dad says in awe as he nibbles on a single worm.

"I can't do it!" Isaac spits out a couple of worms he was trying to swallow. "I give up!"

The crowd suddenly erupts in a gigantic cheer. EJ glances at Faith, who has nearly finished her bowl of worms and will remain the undisputed champion of Dinner Dare—but not if EJ has anything to say about it.

EJ picks up her bowl and dumps the remaining worms in her open mouth; a few worms that don't fit tumble down the front of her shirt. She gulps the worms down in one giant swallow and slams the empty bowl on the table—CRACK!

"Waaaaaahhhhhhhhhhh!" Faith's ear-piercing scream jolted EJ out of her Dinner Dare daydream. She looked down and was happy to see that her bowl was *actually* empty—she hadn't imagined the eating part.

"EJ, don't slam your bowl down." Mom tried consoling Faith as she continued to scream. "You know loud noises like that scare her."

Faith started screaming at even a higher pitch, if that was possible. Bert matched her scream with a howl.

"Sorry, Mom." EJ really was sorry. "Here, I know what will make her stop crying. Isaac, do your thing."

Isaac grinned and leaned toward Faith's high chair, rubbing his finger against the front of his top and bottom teeth. Once he got them good and dry, he tucked his lips up in his gums and said in a high-pitched voice, "Hey, Faith, it's your friend—Lipless Man!"

Faith immediately stopped screaming and stared at Isaac, as if in a trance.

"Lipless Man can't give good kisses," Isaac continued.

"Which is a good thing, because he's got terrible cooties," EJ added.

"But he can nibble on baby fingers!" Faith stuck out her hand toward Isaac, knowing what would come next. Isaac snatched her chubby fingers and gently nibbled on them, making "nom-nom-nom" Cookie Monster sounds, and Faith's face lit up before letting loose with a melodic giggle.

"Delicious!" Lipless Man said. "Thank you for sharing your fingers with me!"

Faith clapped. Mom and Dad joined in, laughing.

"Thanks, Isaac," EJ whispered. He grinned at her.

"So you'll eat baby fingers, but not spaghetti squash, eh, Isaac?" Mom asked.

"I think Faith and EJ might be the only takers for this new wormlike culinary experience," Dad said, biting into a piece of the whole wheat toast. "Isaac and I are both out."

Mom spooned a glob of beef and noodles puree into Faith's mouth. "I think there's a box of mac 'n' cheese in the pantry if you picky Paynes want to make it for your dinner. I always knew girls were more adventurous than boys." Mom winked at EJ.

"Yeah, girls rule and boys—" EJ didn't get a chance to finish her statement because at that precise moment Bert made an impressive vertical jump to knock the beef and noodles jar out of Mom's hand and onto the linoleum floor, where he frantically licked up as much as he could.

"*Bert!* You mangy mongrel!" Dad swooped around Mom and scooped the dog up like a baby. "What has gotten into you?"

"Dad, don't!" EJ didn't like to to see Bert punished almost as much as she didn't like being punished herself. "He's sorry!"

Bert looked up at Dad and licked the remnants of the brown goop off his snout like it was the most delicious thing he'd ever eaten. He didn't look sorry at all. In fact, the way he was twisting his neck to look at the floor where Mom was cleaning up the mess with a paper towel, EJ was sure Bert would do it again if given the chance.

"Matthew Cuthbert T-Rex Payne"—Mom meant business when she used a full name—"you're one more naughty thing away from a trip to obedience school."

Chapter 2
Splash Guard

Dear Diary,

Mom says that every kid needs to know three things: how to make pb 'n' j (a survival skill), how to operate a vacuum (she says this is an essential life skill, but I say it's just a way for her to make her offspring do manual labor as young as possible), and how to swim. Faith's still too little for the first two, but she's just old enough for the "Mommy and Me" swim class at the Spooner YMCA. So us kids and Mom are heading to the Y after school, where we'll all be in the pool at once. Isaac will be in the shallow end with the guppies class, practicing easy things like holding their breaths and proper kicking technique (yawn), Mom and Faith will be splashing on the steps of the shallow end (double yawn), and I will be in the deep end with the rest of the sharks, where we'll be doing the backstroke. (I've been practicing in the bathtub at home between classes, and I'm pretty much the best at it.)

Mom took me to my first swim lesson when I was about Faith's age. Then came tadpoles when I was three, guppies at five, barracudas at seven, dolphins at nine, and sharks at eleven.

And while I've always loved swimming, it was never anything more than just plain old fun for me. That is, until the summer Olympics when I saw Missy Franklin compete on TV. Missy was only seventeen at her first Olympics, Diary—just six years older than me! And she won four gold medals—two of them for backstroke events. She has won countless awards and broken American records and world records. She swims so fast that some people call her "Missy the Missile." Isn't that the best nickname you've ever heard in your life?

But she's not just an amazing athlete. She's a super-cool girl who isn't afraid to talk about her faith. In fact, I read an article once where she was quoted like this: "God is always there for me. I talk with Him before, during, and after practice and competitions. I pray to Him for guidance. I thank Him for this talent He has given me and promise to be a positive role model for young athletes in all sports." See? Super cool!

Basically, Diary, Missy the Missile is amazing. And I want to be just like her when I'm seventeen. And eighteen. And fifty-seven. And one hundred and thirty-two.

So there's no time for messing around, Diary. I've gotta get my head in the game and do some serious training today at the

Y. Look out, swimming world, here I come!

EJ

(Emma Jean, the Swimming Machine)

P.S. Okay, yes, the nickname I've given myself is lamesauce. If I write a letter to Missy Franklin, maybe she'll write me back with a suggestion for a better one!

EJ steps onto the highest spot on the winners' podium and takes a deep breath. Even after years of hard work, she can't believe this is actually happening. A gold medal—the goal she's been working for since she was a little girl. But the truth is, for an Olympic swimmer with talent like EJ's, there are many more goals to reach.

EJ applauds and remembers to smile as the sports coat–wearing Olympic judges hang medals around the necks of the third- and second-place swimmers. Bronze and silver—both competitors should be proud. But neither of those medals would've been enough for EJ. No, for Emma Jean, the Swimming Machine, competing means winning. There is no other option.

She watches in awe as the female judge retrieves the gold medal from a velvet-lined box and approaches the winner's podium. EJ bows at the waist and slips her head through the loop of ribbon. As she stands upright, her heart pounds behind the weight of the golden circle as it rests against her chest. A second judge smiles and hands EJ a beautiful bouquet of flowers. "Thank you," she says as she shakes hands with the judges. She hopes they can read lips, because the roar of the crowd is so loud that they can't possibly hear the words coming out of her mouth. EJ looks up into the stands and sees thousands of smiling faces, American flags rippling through the seats, and hands waving and clapping—all for her. She raises her hands above her head and waves one hand and her flowers at the crowd.

"Ladies and gentlemen," the voice on the loudspeaker says, cutting through the audience noise. "Would you please rise for the playing of the national anthem of the United States of America?"

"EJ, what are you doing up there?" Mom set the diaper bag on the locker room bench that EJ found herself standing on as her Olympic daydream dissolved. She removed her hand from her heart and hopped down.

"Would you be proud of me if I won a gold medal someday?" In two quick motions, EJ slipped off her sweatpants and sweatshirt— revealing her red tank swimsuit with a silver star on the chest.

"I'm already proud of you." Mom unsnapped the buckle of Faith's car seat. "But a gold medal would be pretty amazing."

EJ wadded her clothes and stuffed them into the top cubby in her locker and pulled her red swim cap over her ponytail, fitting it snugly to her head. "I'm ready." She tucked a stray strand of not-quite-brown-but-not-quite-blond hair into the cap. "Is it okay if I go out to the pool deck with my class?"

"Would you help me unbundle Faith first?" Mom reached over and untwisted the shoulder strap on EJ's swimsuit. "I think I might've overdressed her."

EJ looked down at the car seat on the locker room floor and saw the lump of tightly bound miniature winter outerwear: snowsuit, boots, mittens, stocking cap, and two scarves. Only the tiniest bit of a pink button nose and dark eyes peeked out, darting back and forth at the activity of women and girls in the locker room.

"I think you might have overdressed her, too." EJ laughed as she pulled off her sister's stocking cap, resulting in static electricity that made every hair on Faith's head stand straight up—even more than usual. "Faith is a prisoner in her own clothes!"

Faith gave EJ a bright "thank-you" grin as EJ unwound the scarves, revealing the baby's flushed, chubby cheeks. EJ made fast work of releasing Faith from the rest of her clothes before Mom took over to dress the baby in a swimmer diaper and purple flower swimsuit.

"Thanks for your help, EJ." Mom handed Faith a squeaker toy

to gnaw on while she finished getting ready. "Would you please check on Isaac on your way out to the deep end?"

"Aw, Mom, don't worry. He's *fine*." Mom had recently started allowing Isaac to change clothes in the boys' locker room instead of in the family locker room where they could get ready together. "He told me that using the boys' locker room by himself is a big step toward manhood. And the fact that he's there and I'm here means he's not invading my space and bugging me. See? Everybody wins!"

"Just make sure he doesn't need anything, please." Mom smiled, but her tone meant she wasn't kidding. EJ nodded and grabbed her goggles and towel from her locker before flip-flopping to the shower room.

EJ, dressed in her USA-themed racing suit, stands under the showerhead and enjoys the feeling of the jets of hot water hitting her back and arms. The first win came too easy, and now that the medal ceremony is over, her nerves have returned in full force. But the next race, the two hundred–meter backstroke, is her favorite. It's the race that she saw Missy Franklin not only win the gold medal in the London Olympics, but Missy broke the world record for the event, too. Just the thought of it makes EJ shiver with excitement, even in the hot steam of the shower room.

"The best in the world," EJ whispers to herself as she twists the handle of the shower to turn it off. She slings her towel over her shoulder and grabs her Olympic ID badge as she heads to the pool deck. She flashes her ID at the security guard and inhales deeply, comforted by the familiar scent of chlorine. And nerves.

A woman with long chestnut-colored hair stands at the pool's edge, with her back to EJ. The woman is built like a swimmer, tall with broad shoulders and a slim frame, but she's dressed like a coach. That looks just like. . . , *EJ thinks. It is! It's her! EJ's heart pounds in her ears as she realizes it's her swimming inspiration. EJ's glee at actually getting to meet her hero is quickly bubbling up and about to spill over. She tries to play it cool by walking up to the woman and tapping her on the shoulder.*

"Miss Franklin, you are amazing." The woman turns around and EJ throws her arms around her in a bear hug. "You are the reason I got into swimming!"

"Thanks, EJ, but who is Miss Franklin?"

EJ immediately let go of the hug and stepped back to realize she was actually hugging Miss Marla, the Y's head lifeguard and swim teacher for the Mommy and Me class.

"I mean, *Miss Marla.*" EJ tried to shake off the daydream, but Miss Marla *did* look a little bit like Missy Franklin, EJ thought. "Thanks for inspiring kids like me to be better swimmers."

"You're welcome." EJ was glad Miss Marla didn't act like EJ's out-of-the-blue hug was anything too weird. The lifeguard turned her attention back to the preschoolers splashing in the kiddie pool.

EJ was just about to walk toward the deep end when she caught a glimpse of a dad and son coming out of the boys' locker room. *Oh right, I'm supposed to check on the Space Invader.*

"Isaac!" EJ closed her eyes and called through the entry to the boys' locker room. She couldn't actually see into the locker room because there was a privacy wall that you had to walk around to enter or exit, but EJ wasn't going to risk seeing anything she didn't want to see. "Mom wants to know if you're doing okay in there. Do you need anything?"

Silence.

EJ backed against the wall next to the locker room door to get as close as she could and shouted louder. "Isaac Payne! Are you in there?"

The moms and kids already on the pool deck looked in EJ's direction, wondering what the yelling was all about.

"Nothing to see here, folks." She laughed nervously and waved them off. "Everything's under control."

EJ inched as close as she dared in the locker room doorway.

"*Isaac. David. Payne.*" EJ called to him in a harsh whisper, putting some force behind it so her voice would carry past the privacy wall to where Isaac was (hopefully) getting ready. "You're gonna be in a world of hurt when you finally show your face out here, bud!"

Silenter silence.

For half a second, EJ let her mind imagine that maybe Isaac *wasn't* in the locker room. Maybe he got lost. Maybe he wandered away. Maybe. . . .

Just then two identical twin boys strolled out of the locker room—EJ recognized them as barracudas. "Hey!" The boys startled, but then they looked suspicious of the girl standing so close to the door to the boys' locker room. EJ stepped away from the door, hoping it made her look less like a creeper. "Sorry, didn't mean to scare you," she began. "Did you guys see my brother in there?"

The brothers glanced at each other—EJ thought the effect of two face-to-face identical twins dressed in matching trunks was like a 3-D mirror. She started to wonder what it would be like if her mirror image was a real person. . . .

"No daydreams when Isaac is missing, EJ!" she muttered to herself, shaking her head to clear the dream that she'd nearly just slipped into.

"Um, do you mean the kid with the curly blond hair—the guppy?" the twin on the left asked.

EJ's heart lifted. "Yes! That's him. Is he in there?"

"Yeah, he's in there," the other twin replied, giving his brother a funny look. "He's, uh, fine. He should be out in a minute." The boys snickered and walked away.

EJ raised an eyebrow, wondering what the twins' inside joke could be. *Oh well*, she thought, *who* really *understands boys, anyway?* Shaking her head, she turned her attention back to the boys' locker room entrance.

"Everything okay?" EJ spun around to see Mom standing on the pool deck dressed in her royal blue tankini and a black cover-up wrapped around her waist. Faith, perched on Mom's hip, twisted around to watch the activity happening in the pool behind them and squealed excitedly.

"I think so." Even though EJ hadn't been able to fill Mom's request of checking to make sure Isaac had everything he needed, she hoped Mom would just let her join the other sharks and out of Isaac-patrol. "I can't get him to answer me, but some boys told me he's in there."

"Isaac, come out when you're ready," Mom called. "If you hurry, you might have enough time to practice one or two cannonballs before lessons start."

Apparently *cannonballs* was exactly the magic word Isaac needed to hear, because as soon as Mom uttered the word, EJ heard the furious flip-flopping sounds of Isaac making a beeline toward them from somewhere inside the locker room.

A six-year-old-sized blur streaked past EJ to the edge of the pool deck, where he froze in a perfect superhero-style pose—chest out, fists on hips, feet shoulder-width apart, chin in the air. All that was embarrassing enough, but in a split second EJ realized what took Isaac so long to get dressed. Along with his favorite pair of trunks, he also had tied a towel around his neck as a cape (a pretty common occurrence both at swim lessons *and* at home on any given day). Today he'd also added a white mask that looked strangely familiar. . .except EJ couldn't quite figure out what it was.

"Never fear. I have arrived, mortals!" Isaac shouted in his best manly voice. "It is I, the best cannonballer in the universe. . .Splash Guard!"

Every face in the pool area—moms, dads, kids, and lifeguards alike—swiveled to stare at the shouting boy. The sea of eyes looked confused for a moment, but then one of the little tadpoles—a tiny girl with red curls pulled up in two pigtails—pointed at Isaac's face and said, "Mommy, look—underwear!"

EJ gasped. The toddler was right. Isaac had positioned a pair of his tighty-whitey underwear on his head, the waistband loosely around his face and his eyes shining excitedly through the leg holes. To complete the look, he adjusted a pair of goggles over his eyes as the crowd still looked at him in silence, obviously awestruck by the amount of crazy that could be in one little person, EJ thought miserably.

"Buddy, take off the cape first," Mom said, not a hint of embarrassment in her voice.

"I'm not buddy, and I'm not Isaac." He untied the towel cape, let it fall on the green tile floor, and flashed a wide smile. "I'm Splash Guard!"

EJ knew what was coming next. She covered her face with her hands and slunk behind Mom, wishing she had the ability to disappear or teleport or turn invisible—any of those would do.

"Kawabunga!" Splash Guard shouted as he soared off the edge

of the pool into a perfect cannonball, sending a spout of water that soaked four girl barracudas who squealed and complained loudly about getting wet—which EJ thought was just dumb because they were about to have *swim* lessons.

A roar of laughter and applause burst from the onlookers as Splash Guard broke the surface of the water and swam to the edge of the pool. A half dozen other little boys followed Isaac's lead and practiced their cannonballs, too, until Miss Marla blew the whistle, announcing the beginning of lessons.

Relieved the Isaac show was over for now, EJ wondered if there'd ever be a day that she wouldn't have to worry about her brother embarrassing her.

"He's not as bad as you think he is." Mom raised an eyebrow at EJ. "He looks up to you and your vivid imagination—his creativity is just on the outside of his head, and yours is inside."

"I just wish he wouldn't let all the crazy out while I'm around." EJ edged away as Isaac heaved himself out of the pool and sloshed up to Mom.

"That was pretty epic, wasn't it, Marm?" Isaac removed the swim mask and underwear and handed them to Mom before picking up the towel and slinging it over his shoulder.

"Yes, *epic* is a good word for it," Mom said, using her free hand to wring out as much water as she could from the tighty-whities while Faith reached for them. "It'll also be epic if you can wear this wet underwear home without catching your death of cold."

"No problem." Isaac shook the water out of his blond curls like a dog. "I haven't worn underwear for the past three weeks anyway."

Nope, EJ thought as she walked toward the deep end, *I should just plan on being embarrassed for the rest of my life.*

Chapter 3

How to Train Your Dog
(and Your Brother)

Dear Diary,

Bert is undeniably the most ingenious dog I know. He's my best furry friend, sidekick, partner in crime, and he has no equal in the animal kingdom.

Except even I, his biggest fan, have to admit that he's been a horribly bad dog lately.

It's not just the fact that he shredded the rubber part of three pacifiers in one day (honestly, pacifiers *do* look a little bit like dog toys) or that he dug a tube of rash cream out of the baby bag and squeezed it all over the bathroom floor (maybe he had a rash that he wanted to take care of himself), or even that he stole Faith's beef and noodles baby food at dinner a few weeks ago. No, what finally earned Bert a ticket to obedience school was when he ate one of Faith's dirty diapers.

Yes, it's true. Ate. A dirty diaper. (Side note: *Blech!* Bert!

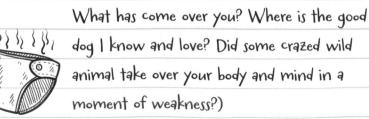

What has come over you? Where is the good dog I know and love? Did some crazed wild animal take over your body and mind in a moment of weakness?)

I've never seen Mom as mad as when she

caught Bert in the act—hiding behind the changing table in the nursery, gnawing on the rancid diaper. I ran in when I heard her scream, and I have to admit that it was so gross that it was all I could do to keep my supper from making a reappearance. Mom must've startled Bert, because he dropped what remained of the diaper and tried to make a run for it. But as much as I wanted to stick up for him, he and I both knew he was in big trouble. Capital BIG.

What followed was the scolding of Bert's life, an extended time-out in his kennel, and baby probation. Except baby probation seems more like a punishment for the humans in the house rather than the dog. Basically we have to keep all of Faith's stuff (and she has a *lot* of stuff) out of his reach. And I'm the one who has to take Bert to obedience school—which wouldn't be so bad, except that it's on Saturday—the one day a week I shouldn't have to think about classes or learning (even Sundays have Sunday school!).

Thanks for nothing, Bert. I hope that diaper gave you a bellyache.

EJ

Click-click. Click-click-click-click.

"Sit. Chewy, sit."

Click-click.

"Come on, sit already!"

EJ watched the young woman with long, curly hair desperately try to coax her tiny chocolate-brown shih tzu to obey the simple command. Except she was using the clicker tool all wrong—definitely not the way the obedience school teacher had told them to do it. EJ wondered if she should say something to her.

"Please, Chewy!" The woman kneeled to put her face down on her pup's level. "Do you want to be nothing more than an obedience-school dropout? Sit!" Chewy attacked her owner's cheek with her pink tongue, and the woman giggled.

EJ looked around the large multipurpose room of the Spooner community center until she found the teacher—a grandpa-aged guy named Mike—who was working one-on-one with a teenage boy and his pony-sized Saint Bernard, Bernie (*Maybe the least-imaginative name for a dog ever,* EJ thought). EJ stifled a giggle as Bernie flattened Mike when the dog made a lunge for the treats that filled the pockets of the instructor's safari vest.

The *click-click*ing and hubbub from about twenty dogs and owners taking the obedience training filled the room with a friendly buzz. Mike had already led the class through a hands-on lecture, and now everyone was supposed to be practicing what they'd learned to get their pets to obey simple commands like sit, stay, and come. EJ was relieved to see that Bert was better at obeying than many of the other dogs in the room. In fact, Bert was a shining star among his classmates—especially compared to whatever was going on with Chewy and her owner.

44

"What do you think, Bertalicious?" EJ pointed at Chewy and the young woman—Chewy now chasing her own tail as her owner laughed and continued clicking the tool for no apparent reason. It looked like she'd given up altogether. "Should we see if we can help them since Mike is busy?"

Bert's tail wagged a yes.

"Hi, I'm EJ. And this is Bert." The young woman stopped clicking and blushed as though she'd been caught doing something wrong. Chewy, a little shy of strangers but also dizzy from spinning in circles, made a motion to run and hide behind her owner's legs but tripped over her own paws and landed in a heap.

"Whoops-a-daisy!" The woman scooped up the ball of fluff and set her upright. Chewy swayed a bit but held steady. "I'm Betsy. And this five pounds of fab is Chewy."

"Is she named after Chewbacca, from *Star Wars*?" EJ kneeled and held out a hand toward Chewy, who sniffed and took a tentative step toward EJ to get a pat on the head, keeping a wary eye on Bert sitting nearby. "Good girl."

"Yep! One of my favorite movies." Betsy fiddled with the clicker in her hand. "Hey, it looked like you and Bert have gotten the hang of this clicker thing. Do you think you could help Chewy and me? We're a hot mess over here."

"Sure!" EJ stood and turned toward Bert. "Mike said the important thing is to use the clicking noise to tell the dog that he has done what you want. So, it's like this. Bert, sit."

Bert looked at EJ, an ornery twinkle in his eye.

"Bert. *Sit*," she said a little more firmly. Bert broke eye contact with EJ and looked up at Betsy and then at Chewy. EJ was going to have to pull out the big guns. "Matthew Cuthbert T-Rex Payne, sit!"

Bert's bottom dropped to the floor immediately when he heard his full name.

The moment Bert sat, EJ gave him a *click-click* and said, "Good boy." She pulled a bacon-flavored treat (his favorite) from her pocket and tossed it Bert's way, but a streak of chocolate-brown fur jumped out of nowhere to intercept the reward. Before EJ even knew what happened, Chewy had swallowed the bacon bite whole.

Bert blinked and looked on the floor for his treat.

"Chewy! Bad girl!" Betsy snatched her pet and scolded her. "*You* didn't earn the treat. Bert did! Oh my goodness, what am I going to do with you?"

EJ kneeled and gave Bert two treats, rubbing his ears the way he liked so much.

"I'm sorry, EJ. Chewy's been all out of sorts since we moved to Spooner two months ago." Betsy sat on the floor and held her pup on her lap. "I read somewhere that dogs sometimes act out when they have big changes in their lives. Change is hard for humans *and* for dogs, isn't it, Chewster?"

Is that why you're squeezing rash cream and eating diapers, Bert? EJ glanced down at her furry friend as she grasped his collar loosely. The truth was, Bert, EJ, and the rest of the Paynes had gone through quite a bit of change since Faith joined the family at the end of the summer. EJ just wanted Bert to be the normal, well-behaved dog she knew and loved; she'd never stopped to wonder *why* he was doing naughty things.

"So I tell Chewy to sit, and I don't click this thing or give her a treat until she actually does it?" Betsy placed the dog on the floor, facing her.

"Right," EJ said. "And then you do it over and over again

until Chewy understands that the clicker means she is obeying correctly."

"Chewy, sit." Two dark eyes looked at Betsy through the dark fluff, but no sitting happened. "Sit!"

"Keep repeating the command firmly," EJ whispered, trying to not distract Chewy.

"Chewy, sit. Sit. Sit, sit, sit!" Betsy's rising volume meant she was getting more and more frustrated. Without warning, Bert pulled away from EJ's grip on his collar, and he trotted to Chewy, stopping next to her.

"Bert!" EJ scrambled to remove him but stopped short when she realized what was happening.

"Chewbacca Lenore Shrider, I said sit your bottom down!"

Chewy's eyes darted to Bert, and Bert's hind end dropped to the ground, as if showing his new friend the ropes of this whole obedience thing. Chewy looked from Bert to EJ and finally to Betsy, the dog's pink tongue hanging out of her mouth and a look of deep concentration in her eyes. Betsy nodded and said, "Yes, Bert's right. Now, sit!"

With all the drama the little dog could muster, Chewy pulled her tongue in her mouth and let out a giant sigh before plopping down.

Click-click went Betsy's clicker. "Good girl!" she squealed, rewarding Chewy with a treat before turning her attention to Bert. "And I think we should share a treat with Bert, too. What a good example he is." Bert happily accepted the reward and trotted back to EJ's side.

"Thank you so much for your help." Betsy gave EJ a warm hug. "We're going to keep practicing *sit*." Betsy had her back to Chewy, so she didn't see that her little dog sat perfectly when she heard the word *sit*.

"Look!" EJ pointed and laughed. "She's a fast learner."

EJ and Bert returned to their spots to practice more commands with the clicker. They'd worked through "come," "stay," and "lie down." Bert was mastering the "speak" command, and a lot of the other dogs in the room were barking as well. EJ was having a hard time concentrating on Bert's bark, especially when she heard the deep, gravelly bark of Bernie the Saint Bernard. She wondered what Bernie's voice would sound like if he were a human. . . .

"Hey, EJ, earth to EJ. I'm over here."

"Wha—?" EJ's neck snaps toward the young man's voice. Except nobody's there. EJ scratches her head. "Hearing voices—never a good sign." She smiles to herself.

"You're not hearing voices. I'm down here!"

EJ looks down to see Bert smiling up at her, tail wagging.

"Bert, you can talk?" EJ can't believe what she's seeing and hearing. She drops down to the floor to sit next to her pooch. "Since when do you talk?"

"Oh, I've always been able to talk." Bert sits and scratches his ear with his back leg casually. "But until now I've just used my excellent dog faces to tell you how I'm feeling."

"You're right. I've always known what you're thinking. . .until recently," EJ says. "So what about it, Bert? What's going on with you? And please explain to me—a dirty diaper?"

Bert lies down with his front paws on EJ's knee.

"Was that too gross?"

"Yes, I think 'too gross' is putting it lightly." EJ thinks for a moment. "So what's the deal? Pacifiers? Rash cream? Beef and noodles?

Do you not like Faith or what?"

"Oh no! Faith is great—I love Faith!" Bert says. "I just. . .well. . .I don't want to say it."

"Bert, you're my best furry friend. Whatever you say won't change that," EJ says. "Spit it out already."

"Well, it's like this, EJ." Bert takes a big breath before he continues. "Before Faith came, I could count on getting attention from everybody in the family. Obviously I'm your dog, so you're my favorite human Payne."

"Obviously." EJ grins.

"But Faith needs a lot of attention because she's a baby—I know she can't feed herself or dress herself or clean herself. But she's hilarious and fun to have around. So it's not just that she's getting attention from Mom and Dad. . . ."

A light bulb flashes on in EJ's brain. "You think Faith has taken your place as the center of attention. . .that she's the new family pet?"

"Some days I think the only way I can get anybody to even notice me is if I do something that will get me into trouble, EJ!" Bert breaks eye contact with EJ and looks embarrassed. "If I get scolded or sent to the kennel, at least you guys know I'm there."

EJ scratches Bert's head, feeling guilty.

"Even though I knew you were bummed that you had to bring me to obedience school today, I was just plain old excited because that meant we would get to spend the whole morning together—just like we used to!" Bert's tail wags a little sadly.

"Aw, Bert. This is all my fault." EJ pulls her pooch onto her lap. "You're right. Faith takes up a lot of our attention. But you're my dog and my friend, and I have to make sure that I'm giving you attention, too."

"*Do you mean it, EJ? Really?*" Bert jumps up and licks EJ's face, his tail wagging excitedly.

"*Yes, I promise.*" EJ crosses her heart with a fingertip. "*But you've got to promise me no more diapers. Deal?*"

Bert yipped happily, and EJ was sure that meant "deal" in Bertspeak.

"Isaac, you'd better come in here and clean up your cars or Dad is gonna be mad!"

EJ had just stepped on a Matchbox car and skidded across the linoleum floor in the kitchen. Just last night Dad had given them both a lecture about cleaning up after themselves and keeping temptations away from Bert and Faith. "And if Faith gets ahold of one of these cars and chews on it, you're gonna be in even bigger trouble!"

"Those aren't mine. *You* clean them up." Isaac's response came from the living room, where he was watching a DVD.

EJ rolled her eyes and took from the pantry two bacon-flavored dog treats for Bert and four Oreos for herself. Isaac was the only one in the family who played with Matchbox cars, so unless a Matchbox car bandit broke into their house and left without cleaning up his toys, it was Isaac's mess to take care of. EJ shut the pantry door and turned to see Bert eyeballing one of Faith's soft chew toys abandoned under the high chair.

"Bert, leave it." EJ used a new command they had learned at obedience school. Bert immediately responded, stepped away from the toy, and looked at EJ with an innocent face. EJ reached in her pocket and gave her friend the reassuring *click-click* sound to tell him that he did the right thing.

"Good boy, Bertie. Come get your reward." Bert eagerly accepted the bacony goodness EJ offered and trotted to his dog bed in the corner of the room for a snooze.

EJ picked up the baby toy and set it on the high chair tray and was just about to pop an Oreo in her mouth when an idea popped into her mind. An idea so brilliant that she couldn't believe she had never thought of it before. Now she just had to put it to the test.

"Isaac, would you come here, please?" EJ figured asking instead of commanding was probably the best way to train a brother.

"I told you, they're not my Matchbox—" Isaac said as he walked into the kitchen but stopped short at EJ's *click-click*. He came, just like she asked.

"Hey, Isaac, have an Oreo." EJ held out a single chocolate-and-cream sandwich to her brother.

"Wow, thanks!" Isaac took the cookie and gobbled it down.

"Would you like some milk?" EJ grabbed two plastic cups from the cabinet, already knowing her brother's answer. Isaac nodded. "Sit."

Isaac hopped up on a stool at the edge of the countertop. *Click-click.* "Here's another cookie to go with your milk."

"Score!"

"Isaac, I know you said those cars aren't yours." EJ poured milk in the cups and slid one toward her brother. "But would you do me a big favor and just pick them up anyway?"

Isaac's eyes drifted to the remaining cookies in EJ's hand and he took a milk-mustache-making gulp from the cup. EJ could almost see him salivating as he wiped the milk from his upper lip with the back of his hand.

"Yeah, okay. I'll put them away." Isaac slid off the stool and quickly picked up the six tiny cars from the floor, stuffing them in his pockets to take to his room. EJ set two more Oreos next to Isaac's milk and grinned at him.

Click-click.

"Good boy—er, I mean—good job, Isaac."

Chapter 4

THE NINJAS OF THE SQUARE TABLE

Dear Diary,

Remember my fourth-grade teacher named Ms. Pickerington?
Remember how it took *all year* for her to warm up to me,
and it wasn't until the very last day of school that I found out
she actually liked me? Thankfully, last year is just a distant
memory, because fifth grade has really turned
out to be amazing. Not only is my best friend,
Macy, in my class this year, but we also have a
fantastically spectacular teacher—Mrs. Smiley. Her
name is pretty much perfect for her because she puts a smile
on my face. She is fun and creative and is always quick to laugh
and give encouragement. (In my very first creative writing essay
in fifth grade, I described two friends as being "kindred spirits,"
and Mrs. Smiley wrote a note in the margin with a big star
that said, "EJ, you are a girl after my own heart—I love *Anne
of Green Gables*, too!" After that, I knew fifth grade was going
to be just fine.) But she also expects a lot from us—that we
are ready to learn and that we will give her our full attention
and our very best effort. And I try my very hardest not to
disappoint her.

In language arts, Mrs. Smiley has been teaching us about

Camelot. King Arthur, Guinevere, Sir Lancelot, and the Knights of the Round Table—the whole thing is so fun because it feels like history, but it's legend. It's a cool mix of near-fact and fiction, complete with royals and castles and dragons and death-defying rescues and defended honor and heroes and villains!

I've never really liked the idea of damsels in distress, Diary. I tend to think that Rapunzel is just lazy for not figuring out a way to escape the tower on her own—and that Sleeping Beauty should fight the urge to lie down for a snooze and just drink a can of Mountain Dew to stay awake. So in my Camelot, Queen Guinevere would never be helpless, relying on dudes to rescue her. In fact, if King Arthur didn't allow her to put on the suit of armor and sit at the Round Table with the other knights, my Guinevere might just start her own medieval club: the Ninjas of the Square Table. Who needs bulky, clanky-janky armor when you can have stealthy, catlike reflexes, nunchucks, and throwing stars?

EJ

EJ bounced the basketball four times before attempting a layup. The orange ball hooked up, up, and right over the basket.

"Aaaaair baaaaall!" CoraLee McCallister sang behind her. "Hurry up, EJ. Mr. Bergan said we can't skip stations, so I have to wait here—completely bored—till you figure out how to get the ball in the hole." CoraLee yawned dramatically.

EJ rebounded her missed shot and took a deep breath. There were two people on the planet who really got under her skin: the first was Isaac (but now that she'd started training him with the dog clicker and Oreos, maybe there was still hope for him); and the second was CoraLee, a tattle-tale-ey, spoiled, know-it-all girly girl who liked to pick on EJ and make fun of her last name (Payne-in-the-neck, giant Payne, major Payne, chronic Payne—EJ had heard them all). EJ and her family had secretly helped give the McCallister family a Christmas over a year ago when CoraLee's dad had been laid off from his job. EJ was still glad the Paynes had helped the McCallisters, and EJ and CoraLee had even worked together last summer at church camp, but sometimes—like now—EJ wondered if CoraLee would ever stop being mean.

"EJ, your basketball skills are Paynefully pathetic! Shoot. The. Ball!"

"Hey, CoraLee, those words aren't encouraging to EJ." Mr. Bergan, the Spooner Elementary phys ed teacher, caught CoraLee off guard, and EJ saw her blush. If there was one thing CoraLee hated, it was being called out by a teacher. "How about you try again?"

"What I was saying was, shoot the ball, EJ—you can do it!" The blushing CoraLee tried to make a quick recovery in front of the teacher, but Mr. Bergan wasn't fooled at all. "That's better. CoraLee, why don't you come help me hang up some jump ropes and Hula-Hoops from kinder-gym class, and then you can come back into the obstacle course rotation?"

EJ and CoraLee both knew jump rope and Hula-Hoop duty was a mild punishment for the unkind words the teacher had heard come from CoraLee's mouth. "Yes, sir," she mumbled, but then whispered so Mr. Bergan couldn't hear, "This isn't over, royal Payne." EJ waved and stuck her lower lip out in a mocking sad face at CoraLee as she followed Mr. Bergan.

Without the pressure of CoraLee taunting her to make a basket, EJ was able to make a layup easily. She set the basketball in the rack along the wall and took a moment to enjoy the hubbub as her twenty-two classmates played at stations set up around the gymnasium. From basketball and tumbling on mats to jumping through hoops and double-dutch, there really was something for everyone.

As she followed the masking tape arrow on the floor to the next activity station, she was happy to see that it was one of her favorites: beanbag launchers. These crazy contraptions looked like small teeter-totters that you would load a beanbag on one end and then stomp on the other end to send the beanbag up in the air, finally catching the projectile on the way down. Students were supposed to launch and catch the beanbag five times before moving on.

EJ's best friend, Macy Russell, was at one of the launchers. As EJ took a spot at the empty launcher next to her, Macy gave a colossal stomp, and the beanbag soared a good ten feet in the air.

"Nice one, Mace!" EJ grinned.

"Wha—?" Macy startled and her attention swiveled from the beanbag to EJ. "Oh, hey, EJ!"

Thunk. The beanbag landed squarely on Macy's athletic-shoed foot. "I don't think I could've done that if I *tried!*" Macy said. "I wish I could stick the landing in my gymnastic events half as well as this beanbag just did." The girls laughed.

Soon the friends were locked in a contest to see who could launch their beanbag higher. EJ seemed to have the raw strength needed to get maximum height, but Macy had amazing accuracy— it turned out she actually *could* get a beanbag to land on her foot if she tried. Or her head. Or even EJ's head.

"It's too bad there's no career potential in beanbag launching," Macy said. "If there was, you could add it to your list of things you want to do when you grow up."

"Well, we *could* defend a castle with these catapults," EJ said. "There have to be castles that need defending somewhere. Like Camelot. . . ."

"I dub thee Dame Macy, order of beanbag, first class, a Ninja of the Square Table. And I am Dame EJ, heir of the Royal Payne dynasty, first class, a Ninja of the Square Table."

"It's an honor to serve alongside you, Dame EJ." Macy adjusts her black ninja mask so she can see clearly through the eye opening.

"Our goal today is the same as it is every day, my fellow Ninjas of the Square Table." EJ addresses the crowd of stealthy black-wearing individuals gathered around her. She motions to the thick stone wall fortress they're all standing in front of. "And that goal is to protect the people of Camelot from enemies who mean to do us harm."

The ninjas peer silently at their beloved home. Merchants in the square selling fresh produce and goods. Children skipping through the streets singing folk songs. Old men playing a game of chess around the edge of the fountain. Their beloved King Arthur ruling justly from his throne.

"All of these things can be gone in a second if we let the wrong person past the fortress gate." The ninjas' bright eyes turn back to their leader. EJ sees their determination and—even more than that—dedication. "What say you, my friends?"

"I speak for all of us, because as ninjas they are silent," Dame Macy replies. "We join with you, Dame EJ, your Royal Payneness." As if on cue, the ninjas press their pointer fingers to their masks in the "hush" gesture and bow reverently. EJ smiles, nods, and pulls her ninja mask down to cover her face.

"You guys are hogging the beanbag launchers." CoraLee's shrill voice sliced through the daydream. "Let me have a turn!"

"Who goes there?" Dame EJ calls out, motioning to her ninja soldiers to load ammunition into the catapults. "Ye shall not gain entry to Camelot without the proper permission."

"What are talking about you, you weirdo?" CoraLee huffed. "Okay, fine, I'll play along in your bizarre little game." She continued, mumbling, "'Tis I, Princess CoraLee of the kingdom of, um, Spooner."

EJ rolled her eyes, convinced that CoraLee must have the smallest imagination of anyone she knew.

"Princess CoraLee of Spooner, you have been found guilty of insults, bullying, and general tattle-taleyness." EJ peers off the edge of the wall at the princess, dressed in the puffiest bubblegum-colored ball gown she's ever seen. "But the king is a forgiving king, and if you will promise to change your ways, he will grant you entry to Camelot."

"How dare you accuse me of such things?" Princess CoraLee's dress quivers as her temper tantrum gains strength. "You—you are nothing more than a servant! So why don't you fetch my slippers, servant? Do it NOW!"

"Mr. Bergan! EJ and Macy won't let me—"

"Fire!" At least forty rocks soar through the air toward Princess CoraLee, who immediately runs in the opposite direction.

Tweeeeeeeet! "Time to clean up and head back to class," Mr. Bergan called out.

"Camelot is safe for another day." Macy picked up her beanbag launcher and propped it on her shoulder.

"Well done, Dame Macy." EJ grinned at her friend and pressed her finger to her lips.

Chapter 5

DOWN ON ONE KNEE

Dear Diary,

Sometimes (okay, *most* of the time) it feels like there's nothing to do in Spooner during the winter. When the deep freeze sets in and temperatures dip to the single digits (on a warm day), we can't be outside for more than two minutes without turning into kidsicles. So it's indoor activities for a solid four months of the year here in Wisconsin.

Today we're going to one of my favorite places in Spooner: Billy and Bobby's Bowl-a-Rama. (Isn't that a fantastic name for a bowling alley?) Billy and Bobby are grandpa-aged identical twins who have lived in Spooner their whole lives. And when I say *identical* I mean *identical.* They dress alike, talk alike, and I'm pretty sure they each know what the other is thinking. There's a legend that the two boys spent their entire third-grade year at Spooner Elementary pretending to be each other, tricking the teachers so that some days Billy sat at Bobby's desk and vice versa, and they'd intentionally get bad grades on each other's homework—but nobody could tell them apart enough to be able to catch them in the act. I don't know if I believe it or not, but it's a pretty good story anyway.

The best thing about going bowling today is that my favoritest neighbor and second-favoritest neighbor, Mrs. Winkle and Mr. Johnson, are going, too! It's going to be a girls versus boys battle: Mom, Mrs. Winkle, and me against Dad, Mr. Johnson, and Isaac. Faith will be there to cheer (or shriek and blow raspberries, more likely) both teams on. But let's be real, Diary, the boys will be no match for us. Mrs. Winkle bowls on a league of retired teachers, and she has bowled not one but two perfect games in her life. She even has her photo up on the "300 Club" board at the Bowl-a-Rama, where she's wearing a neon-yellow bowling shirt that says "Livin' la Vida '80s" across the front. ("We were celebrating our favorite decade—the 1980s were a decade of thrilling colors, dear," Mrs. Winkle told me.)

For the boys' team, today will be the first time Isaac has ever bowled without bumpers, so I'm betting that at least his first three frames will be gutter balls. (I will *try* not to laugh. But I'm sure I will.)

EJ

EJ stood in front of the rows of colorful balls, looking for the perfect shade of red. Soon she spotted a nice pearly one on the bottom row.

"Aw, rats—sixteen pounds!" EJ knew better than to try to pick up a ball that heavy. At Macy's tenth birthday party, EJ had tried bowling with a beautiful red fifteen-pounder and had almost ended up with a broken foot.

"EJ, the kid balls are over here!" Isaac waved at EJ from across the room. "Look at this *Star Wars* one I found!" Sure enough, Isaac had a hand on a black bowling ball that had an intricate pattern of stars and the movie logo on it.

"Nice!" EJ hoped she'd be able to find one as cool.

"But wait, there's more." Isaac lifted the ball from the rack to reveal a picture of Darth Vader's head on the opposite side of the ball. "The force is strong within this ball. *(Inhale, exhale.)* Luke, I am your bowling ball. *(Inhale, exhale.)*"

EJ grinned at her brother's goofiness. Sure, he was a spaz, but at least he was a spaz with good movie tastes.

"You kids find what you're looking for?" Billy—or was it Bobby?—called to EJ and Isaac from behind the shoe counter a few feet away.

"I found the perfect one for me!" Isaac hefted his *Star Wars* ball and galloped to the two alleys where the adults and Faith were waiting to get started.

"I, well. . ." EJ's eyes scanned the handful of kids' balls left on the rack. Yellow *(bleh)*, orange *(ugly)*, blue *(maybe, but only as a last option)*, and bright pink *(no way, Jose!)*.

"I can see you are a woman of discerning tastes, EJ. Bobby"— EJ made a mental note that the one speaking now must be Billy— "shall we let her choose from our secret stash?"

EJ's eyes brightened. *Secret stash* sounded promising.

"Brother Billy, I believe we shall." Bobby produced a key and unlocked a cabinet door on the front of the shoe counter. The door swung open, and EJ's jaw dropped. The amount of bling radiating from the balls in the secret stash was almost blinding. In a split second EJ knew which one she would pick: the extra-shiny, extra-sparkly red ball with thousands of stars on it. It was so bright that it actually looked like it had been dipped in the sparkles that Mom used for crafts in kids' church.

"That one has your name all over it, EJ girl." Mrs. Winkle peered into the cabinet over EJ's shoulder while EJ carefully picked up the bowling ball. "Billy and Bobby must see something special in you. They don't let just *anyone* into their secret stash, do you, boys?"

"No, ma'am." Side by side, the brothers responded together and hooked their thumbs through the belt loops on their jeans.

"Thank you for trusting me with such a beautiful ball." EJ smiled at the brothers and realized she'd lost track of which one was which again. "I will be very careful with it."

Mrs. Winkle put her arm around EJ's shoulder to guide her to the lanes where the family was waiting.

"Well, don't be *too* careful with it," the brother on the left called, a twinkle in his eye.

"Yeah, I mean, you're about to throw it across the room with the intention of knocking things over," the other twin said. "So throw 'er with gusto!"

EJ set her ball in the ball return and finally got a good look at Mrs. Winkle's bowling outfit: white pants with tiny, multicolored bowling balls and pins embroidered all over them, bowling shoes covered with emerald-green sequins, a tiny bowler hat pinned to the top of her head, and a button-down collared shirt with what looked like handwritten Magic Marker *X*s all over them.

"Love the outfit, as always, Wilma," Mom said, echoing exactly what EJ was thinking. Mrs. Winkle wore the most fascinating outfits—often they were looks she designed herself. "But what's with the shirt?"

"It's my lucky strike shirt, dear!" Mrs. Winkle laughed. "Every time I knock over all ten pins, I add an *X* to celebrate a strike!"

Mrs. Winkle's unique and creative style was one of the many things EJ loved about her grandmother-y neighbor. Since EJ's grandparents, Nana and Pops, lived far away in Ohio, it was great having a friend like Mrs. Winkle nearby.

"Hope you Paynes like nachos, because I just ordered two plates of them," Mr. Johnson said as walked with his cane from the snack counter. Until a little more than a year ago, Mr. Johnson only used his gruff voice to yell at neighborhood kids to get off his property and stay away from his flower garden and birdhouses, or else! But he'd abandoned his role as lonely neighborhood grouch and had found a place to belong with Mrs. Winkle and the Payne family.

"Sounds delicious, Lester. I'm sure we'll love them," Dad said, tying a double knot in his left bowling shoe. "Are we ready to get started, then?"

"Just a minute, I forgot to change shoes." Mr. Johnson slipped his feet out of his loafers and into his rented bowling shoes. He used the armrest of his chair to ease himself onto one knee to tie the shoe.

At precisely the same moment, Mrs. Winkle turned from the computer score-keeping screen, where she and Isaac had been typing everyone's names. When she saw a kneeling Mr. Johnson, she gasped.

"Oh, Lester!" Mrs. Winkle covered her mouth with her hands

and her eyes shimmered. "I knew this day would be coming soon. I just didn't imagine it would be *today!*"

EJ wondered what on earth was wrong with Mrs. Winkle. Was she about to cry? Mom and Dad raised their eyebrows at each other and she saw Dad give Mom a thumbs-up on the sly.

Mr. Johnson cleared his throat uneasily and looked mildly terrified.

"Of course, it makes sense that you'd do it now," Mrs. Winkle continued, as if she were thinking out loud. "I mean, we're here with the people who mean the very most to us—and who brought us together."

EJ scrunched her forehead, trying to make sense of what Mrs. Winkle was going on about. She felt a tug on her sleeve.

"EJ, what's happening?" Isaac whispered.

"Shh, I'm trying to figure it out," EJ replied.

"But I love you, and you love me." Mrs. Winkle was getting giddier and talking faster with every word. "We love each other. And we will be so happy together. And, let's face it, we're not getting any younger. So, Mr. Lester Johnson, you don't even have to ask the question. The answer is yes. Yes. Yes!" Mrs. Winkle clapped her hands and laughed gleefully.

"Excuse me. *What* question?" Isaac's patience for the mystery had obviously run its course.

Mr. Johnson took his time to finish tying his second bowling shoe. "Wilma, you're a brilliant woman with extreme style, and you'll always outshine me," he began, pulling a small velvet box from his pants pocket. "And you've already stolen my thunder, but you've said all the things that are on my heart better than I could've said them."

Oh! EJ thought. *I've seen a scene like this in movies!*

"So even though you've already told me the answer to my question, I will ask it anyway." Mr. Johnson took a deep breath and smiled up at Mrs. Winkle as he opened the box to reveal a diamond ring. "Wilma Winkle, will you marry me?"

EJ takes one final moment to make sure everything's in place. Normally she wouldn't wear anything so completely girly—a floor-length dress with enough sparkle to light up a room—but it's not every day that she gets to star in Mrs. Winkle's wedding as the flower girl.

Okay, maybe she isn't exactly the star of the wedding, but after the bride and groom, she has to get next billing, right?

EJ makes sure the glittering star-shaped confetti is present and accounted for in the flower girl basket, lifts a gloved hand to straighten the jewel-encrusted tiara on her head, adjusts her balance in her kitten-heel shoes, and takes a deep breath.

She hears the first notes of her music cue from inside the Vine Street Community Church auditorium and takes a confident step down the aisle. All eyes are on EJ as she delicately scatters dazzling sparkles down the aisle, creating the perfect pathway for the bride to follow.

"Isn't she a perfectly elegant flower girl?" someone whispers.

"Wilma made the right choice choosing EJ," comes the reply.

EJ smiles, and she times her steps and confetti placement as the music swells. She can feel the admiration of all the guests wishing they could be as lovely.

"Eeeeeeeeebababababah!" The dinosaur-like screech coming out of Faith's mouth rudely snapped EJ out of her daydream. Mom held Faith in her lap while the baby pulled Kleenexes out of Mrs. Winkle's purse gleefully, tossing them into the air and watching them drift to the ground.

"EJ, did you hear Mrs. Winkle ask Faith to be the flower girl in the wedding?" Mom bounced Faith on her knee and got her to giggle.

EJ's stomach dropped to her toes, and her breath caught in her chest. Ever since Mr. Johnson and Mrs. Winkle had started courting, she'd assumed, counted on, and dreamed about being the flower girl at their wedding.

"I thought Faith could use some practice—but I think we've discovered she's a natural." Mrs. Winkle watched Faith pull out another Kleenex and toss it. "And, EJ, I want you to be my junior bridesmaid. Please say that you will."

EJ's stomach did a flop from her toes, up to generally where it should be. Junior bridesmaid—that sounded like it could be even more important than flower girl.

"As junior bridesmaid, you'll get to help me plan the wedding, wear a fabulous dress, and stand on stage beside me during the ceremony," Mrs. Winkle said. "And. . .I was wondering if you would be willing to learn 'You Are My Sunshine' on your ukulele so you can play and sing it when I walk down the aisle. Would you like that?"

EJ stomach flipped again—this time out of excitement instead of disappointment.

"I'd love it!" EJ gushed, throwing her arms around Mrs. Winkle's neck in a hug. "I'll answer the same way you did to Mr. Johnson. Yes. Yes!"

"Of course, we'd like you to officiate the ceremony, Reverend Payne." Mr. Johnson's eyes sparkled as he addressed Dad with the uncharacteristic formal title. Everybody at church just called him David. Or sometimes Pastor David.

"It'll be my honor, Lester." Dad shook Mr. Johnson's hand and pulled him in for a hug.

EJ could see the wheels turning in Isaac's brain. Apparently he didn't have a role in the wedding yet, and he wasn't about to be left out.

"Hey, Mr. Johnson." Isaac squeezed himself between Mr. Johnson and Dad as their hug broke up. "If it's okay with you, I'd like to be the stand-up comedian in the wedding."

"Um. . ." Mr. Johnson looked to Mrs. Winkle for help, but she just gave him an encouraging wink. "Well, Isaac, would you be willing to audition for it?"

"Sure!" Isaac's face lit up. "Right now?"

"Okay, yes, right now." Mr. Johnson tried to look official, but the corners of his mouth gave away his amused grin.

"EJ, would you please be my assistant for this audition?" EJ groaned at Isaac's request. She could see what was coming—her brother still only knew one joke that she'd heard no fewer than 6,438 times in her life.

"Isaac, I don't wan—" EJ stopped short when she saw the look of disapproval on Dad's face. "All right. Go."

Isaac cleared his throat.

Isaac: What kind of cats like to go bowling?
EJ: What are you talking about? Cats don't bowl.
Isaac: It's the joke, EJ. What kind of cats like to go bowling?
EJ: Wait a second. Are you telling a joke that's *not* your "Noah good joke" one?
Isaac: Yes. So answer the question. What kind of cats like to go bowling?

EJ: I don't know.

Isaac: Alley cats.

Adults: [laugh]

Faith: [squeals]

EJ: [shocked silence]

Isaac: EJ, do you get it? Bowling? *Alley* cats—

EJ: Yeah, I get it. I'm just too stunned to laugh because I never thought you'd ever tell a new joke in your life.

Isaac: It was time for a change.

Mr. Johnson: [still laughing] I never knew I wanted a stand-up comedian at my wedding till now. Isaac, you're hired!

Chapter 6

ROBO BABY

Dear Diary,

Macy and I signed up for "infant home care certification" training at the Spooner Red Cross, and today is the day for the class! How cool and official will it be to introduce myself as "EJ Payne, infant home care professional"? (Okay, okay, it's basically a fancy term for a babysitter, but "infant home care professional" sounds so much more legit, right?) If the teacher doesn't give me a badge or at the very least an ID card, I might just have to make one myself to keep in my wallet so I can pull it out to impress people now and then—a photo ID framed by multicolored stars and using lots of different fonts to highlight my babysitting expertise.

CoraLee overheard Macy and me talking about the babysitting class at recess the other day, and in typical CoraLee fashion, she had to come stick her nose in our conversation and ruin it by telling us that she was signed up for the class, too.

CoraLee: Mom says it'd be a good idea for me to get certified, which I think is just plain dumb because I've been babysitting my little sister for six months now.

Macy: You never know, CoraLee, maybe you'll learn

something useful in class.

Me: Yeah, CoraLee, it's probably a lot different babysitting an infant than babysitting your sister, Katy. I mean, she's in first grade. She's potty trained and can pretty much take care of herself, right?

CoraLee: EJ, you've never babysat before. Don't talk about things you don't know anything about.

Me: You mean Katy's *not* potty trained? Well, that's awkward.

CoraLee: Just wait till Saturday, P-A-I-N. We'll see who makes the better babysitter!

Me: You're on.

The description of the class on the Red Cross website says that we'll be trained with "lifelike infant simulators." Mom says those are probably baby dolls that have computer chips in them, and we'll have to do things like change diapers, feed, soothe, and rock them. Truthfully, "lifelike infant simulators" sound a bit too much like robots to me. Lots of kids (my brother included) think robots are cool. I, on the other hand, do not. I don't trust things that seem like they can think for themselves, but they don't actually have a brain. (Transformers will take over the world someday—you heard it here first, Diary!) But if these things are cute, cuddly baby dolls, how bad could they really be?

EJ

EJ leans over the edge of the cradle and watches the sweet baby boy named Abner sleep. She slips her pointer finger in the baby's fist and marvels at his perfectly formed, tiny fingers and fingernails. Her eyes drift to his angelic face: long eyelashes, chubby cheeks, light hair as soft as the feathers on a baby chick. She is the very best babysitter in the whole world.

Abner stirs slightly in his sleep, and a tiny pink tongue peeks out of the corner of his mouth.

"What are you dreaming of, silly baby?" EJ murmurs, smiling to herself. "A giant bottle filled with warm milk?"

Abner yawns and stretches, waking up from his nap slowly. His bright green eyes, groggy at first, quickly focus on EJ's face, and his mouth splits open in an adorably toothless grin.

"Hey there, handsome guy!" EJ picks up Abner and hugs him close, enjoying his powder-fresh smell. "Did you have a good snooze?"

"Waaaahhh-aaaaaaaaaahhhhhh. Waaaaaahhhhhhhhhh!" EJ's babysitting dream whisked away, and she nearly dropped the screaming piece of baby-shaped rubber in her arms. She looked around the Red Cross classroom at the dozen other students going for their infant home care certification, and she realized her baby was the only one crying.

"Shh. Come on, little guy, it's okay." EJ tried pushing Abner's pacifier in his mouth, but the horrible sound continued to come from the speaker somewhere on his body. It was actually pretty impressive how much sound it could put out.

EJ felt panic rise in her chest, and she looked at her classmates to see if anyone else was doing something helpful that she could try. Each student was standing at a spot along a row of long tables, interacting with an infant simulator doll and various baby supplies—diapers, blankets, bottles, toys. EJ saw Macy changing the diaper of her baby—a newborn doll named Gretchen. CoraLee was feeding a bottle to her doll—a four-month-old named Penelope. The rest of the students were older girls EJ had seen before, but they were already in middle school, and she didn't know any of their names. EJ thought it was too bad there weren't any boys in the class, but then she had another thought: the fewer certified babysitters there were in Spooner, the better chance she had at making some real money. (And she needed a new bike for the summer!)

"Waaaaaahhhhhh!" Abner wasn't letting up.

"What's wrong with you, baby?" EJ muttered. As Abner's cry got louder, she held the wailing infant simulator at arm's length to keep the source of the earsplitting sound as far from her ears as possible.

"EJ, use baby's name when you talk to baby." The voice of the instructor named Miss Debbie rose above Abner's cries. "And don't forget—baby needs head and neck support!"

"Oh, right. Sorry, ma'am." EJ glanced down at her *Babysitting 101* handbook to check the proper holding technique and pulled Abner to her, his head and neck resting comfortably in the crook of her arm. "There, Abner. Is that better?"

"Waaaaaahhhhhhhhhhhaaaaaaaahhhhhhhhh!" Was it possible the pitch of the cry had jumped an entire octave? How much louder would it get?

"Shh. Shhhh. Hush now, Abner. I am here." EJ began to rock the doll in a steady rhythm, hoping desperately that's what he wanted. If Miss Debbie was already grading students on their performance, she was definitely getting some less-than-awesome marks right now.

"You're a natural, Mace." EJ gently bounced the screeching Abner in her arms as she walked to her friend. "How am I supposed to know if I'll make a good babysitter with a nightmare of a kid like this?" Abner hiccupped and screamed more earnestly. "Sorry, I don't really mean *nightmare*," EJ reassured the crying doll, just in case it understood what she was saying.

"We just have to figure out what he needs, EJ." Macy gently set the contented Gretchen in her car seat and turned to help her best friend. "May I?"

"No, I need to do it myself." EJ raised her voice over the robo baby's wailing. "Could you just walk me through it, please?"

"Let's see. Diaper?"

"Clean."

"Hungry?"

"Fed him"—EJ checked the clock on the wall—"eight minutes ago."

"Well, he just must want to be close to you." Macy held up her wrist where she wore a bracelet with the computer key that matched Gretchen's computer interface. EJ wore a similar key on her wrist—for Abner. "That key on your wrist means that you're the only one he'll respond to."

"You're right, I can do this." EJ lifted Abner's baby-blue shirt and touched her key to the sensor on his back. His cries immediately dropped in strength and volume, and by the time she was rocking him a few moments later, his whimpering had all but stopped.

"Thank *goodness*." CoraLee rolled her eyes and made sure EJ could hear the annoyance in her voice—from all the way across the room. "I think some people should realize they aren't cut out to be babysitters."

EJ felt heat rush to her cheeks.

"Don't listen to CoraLee," Macy whispered. "You're doing fine."

Gretchen started to cry, and Macy picked her up from the car seat. But before Macy could get Gretchen's crying under control, Abner started to scream again.

"Here it comes, girls." Miss Debbie was a little too excited about crying baby dolls. "The empathy cry!"

A few seconds later, the infant simulator of the student next to Macy started screaming. Then the next and the next, until every baby in the room was wailing at the top of his or her lungs—er— speakers?

. . .Except for CoraLee's baby, Penelope, who lay perfectly contented in her babysitter's arms, not making a peep. The look on CoraLee's smug, judge-y face made it obvious to EJ that CoraLee really did think she was better than everyone else.

Even though EJ wanted nothing more than to snatch the smug look off CoraLee's face, she knew that getting her certification was more important, so she focused her attention back on Abner.

"CoraLee, I need to check something on your infant simulator." Miss Debbie didn't seem to be fazed by the vortex of crying around them.

"Please, ma'am, she's so content right now." CoraLee rubbed the baby doll's back gently. "I'd rather not disturb her."

"Well, I'm pretty sure nothing could disturb Penelope right now, CoraLee." Miss Debbie lifted Penelope's shirt and checked the small LED display on the doll's back. "Just as I thought. Penelope's battery is dead." Miss Debbie turned and walked straight to the supply closet to find a working doll for CoraLee.

"What? You can't be serious!" With Miss Debbie otherwise

occupied, CoraLee dropped Penelope onto the table in front of her and scowled at the doll. "So none of what I've been doing for the past thirty minutes even *counts?*"

"Baby needs head and neck support, CoraLee!" EJ matched her voice to be as singsongy as Miss Debbie's. CoraLee's eyes shot daggers at EJ, and EJ smiled brightly at CoraLee while she fed a quieting Abner a bottle.

"Here's baby Jack for you, CoraLee." Miss Debbie emerged from the supply closet and entered a code on the back of the roly-poly baby Jack with freckles and a cowlick that made the hair on the back of his head stand straight up. Once activated, Miss Debbie handed the baby and his computer key bracelet to CoraLee, and Jack immediately started crying like he'd been saving up all his good wailing and shrieking for months.

EJ put a contented Abner on her shoulder and patted his back until she heard a *burp* followed by a lovely little *coo*.

"There's a good baby, Abner." EJ adjusted the doll in her arms and smiled down at him. "See? I knew I could do it. I'll make an excellent babysitter."

By now, the rest of the students had been able to calm their babies down—that is, all but CoraLee's Jack, whose cry had turned from sounding sad to frustrated to furious in a matter of moments. CoraLee's face drained of all its color as she tried all the tricks she knew to get him to stop crying.

"Okay, girls, it's time to learn the infant choking procedure on your babies." Miss Debbie raised her voice above Jack's cry.

Finally CoraLee found what Jack wanted, because his angry shrieks subsided to just pathetic whimpers. CoraLee wiped sweat from her forehead with a spare burp cloth.

Miss Debbie demonstrated the proper technique for first aid on a choking infant by placing a spare doll facedown on her arm. ("Head and neck support, girls!" she said.) Then she used the heel of her hand to hit the doll on the back until the airway was cleared.

"Now you try." Miss Debbie walked around the room with her clipboard, making notes as she observed students.

EJ made sure that she was doing every step exactly the way Miss Debbie showed them. "Excellent work, EJ." Miss Debbie smiled at her and made a note on the clipboard. "Ten out of ten on this one."

EJ propped Abner's head on her shoulder and held him with one arm as she flipped through her babysitting handbook, reviewing the things Miss Debbie said would be on the written test, while the rest of the class continued to practice with the dolls.

"Okay, CoraLee, your turn." EJ looked up to see Miss Debbie grading CoraLee's infant choking procedure. CoraLee confidently placed the baby facedown on her arm. (Even EJ had to admit she did a great job supporting Jack's head.) Then she quickly and efficiently began giving back blows. "Very good!" Miss Debbie smiled. But on the fifth *thump*, Jack's head flew away from his body like a rocket ship blasting off. The softball-sized, brown-haired, brown-eyed object arced through the air—seemingly in slow motion—spinning so fast that it almost made EJ dizzy.

With the reflexes of a much younger woman, Miss Debbie dodged the projectile head.

CoraLee gasped and covered her mouth with her hand, horrified.

EJ watched, speechless, as the head hit the floor and rolled toward her, under tables, and past other students, coming to rest inches from her toes. Some of the older girls burst into laughter and pointed at CoraLee.

EJ picks up the doll head and shakes her head in mock sadness.

"Poor little Jack," she says with a pout in her voice. "What did you ever do to Miss CoraMean to deserve this?"

EJ tosses the head to CoraLee and smirks. "Some people should realize they aren't cut out to be babysitters."

EJ tried to suppress a grin that tickled the corners of her mouth. Even though it was just in a daydream, giving CoraLee a taste of her own medicine felt pretty good. Cradling Jack's head in her free hand, she walked across the room and held it out toward an embarrassed CoraLee, red-faced and on the verge of tears.

"Don't worry," EJ quietly assured CoraLee. "I'm not an expert babysitter yet, but I'm pretty sure the heads don't *actually* come off."

CoraLee took the head from EJ, her eyes still threatening to spill tears.

"And I know you're a good babysitter," EJ said quietly. "So don't let a crazy robo baby make you think you're not."

"Yeah, okay." CoraLee's face softened a bit, and her eyes dried. "Thanks, EJ. You will probably make an okay babysitter, too."

That might be the nicest thing she's ever said to me, EJ thought. *I'll take it.*

Chapter 7

THE BOY WHO SNORED WOLF

Dear Diary,

My overnight bag is packed with a toothbrush, toothpaste, and a brand-new pair of pajamas. I've got a Ziploc bag filled with a dozen fresh-baked Cowboy Cookies, and I'm ready for a sleepover at Macy's house!

Sleepovers are one of my very favorite things. Especially when they are at someone else's house, so I can relax knowing that the Space Invader won't show up in his Darth Vader helmet and scare everyone to death (like he did during my ninth birthday sleepover) or that Faith's 2:00 a.m. dinosaur-like screeches for food or a diaper change or some other unknown reason won't wake us up. No, at this point in my life, it's better to have sleepovers as far away from the Payne house as possible.

It's just going to be Macy, her mom, and me tonight. Macy's dad is in Milwaukee this weekend for his job, and Bryan, Macy's sixteen-year-old brother, is spending the night at a friend's house. Sometimes Macy complains about Bryan (he's really into science and math. Even when he's around, he usually keeps to himself. In fact, I don't think I've heard him say more than three words in a row), but there's *no way* an older brother could be worse than a younger brother-slash-pest. Sometimes

I wish I could *pay* Isaac to stop talking—just so I could hear myself think. Dad says Isaac sometimes suffers from diarrhea of the mouth. Which I said sounds plain disgusting, but Dad said it just means that sometimes Isaac just gets so excited about something that he can't stop talking. (A problem that *could* be fixed with duct tape, if Mom and Dad would just let me try.)

On the agenda for tonight's sleepover:

1. Pizza. I'm planning on stuffing myself silly. I wonder how many pieces of pizza I can eat.

2. Pop. Only the clear kind, with no caffeine. We're supposed to get at least *some* sleep. We'll see.

3. Cookies. (See #1 re: stuffing myself.)

4. Manicures/pedicures. Normally I'm not allowed to paint my nails, but Mom said it's perfectly allowable for sleepover fun.

5. Movie. Macy recently finished reading *Anne of Green Gables* for the first time, so I'm going to introduce her to the splendidly fantastic and utterly lovely movie that's based on the book. Mom said she was only eight years old when she first saw it, so obviously the movie is *super* old. But it doesn't really matter because the story takes place a long

time ago anyway. I love the movie almost as much as I love
the book (which is a lot).

EJ

EJ never could've imagined there were so many shades of red in the universe.

"How do I pick one when I love them all?" EJ held up two bottles of nail polish and compared them side by side. "Fire engine red or brick red? Or what about that rose-red or the one with the gold flecks in it?"

Macy squinted at the bottles, considering EJ's options. "Well, you have ten fingers and ten toes. What about a different shade of red on each?"

"Macy, you're a genius!" EJ unscrewed the top of a bottle of a particularly bright shade to get a better look at it. "This one reminds me of the color of Red Riding Hood's cape. And that one with the sparkles reminds me of Dorothy's ruby slippers in *The Wizard of Oz*."

Macy's mom worked part-time as a nail tech at a salon in Spooner, so she had shoe boxes full of colors the girls could choose from. The three of them sat at the Russells' kitchen table, Mrs. Russell almost done with Macy's base color on her fingernails—a pale sky blue.

"Mom, would you paint white stripes on my pinkies?" Macy placed her fingers under the drying fan. "And a cute little bird on my thumbnails?"

Mrs. Russell nodded and smiled. "Sounds like my daughter is ready to celebrate spring on her fingers."

"You guessed it!" Macy peeked at her nails under the fan. "It's been a loooong winter."

"In that case"—Mrs. Russell rummaged through a shoe box and produced a trio of pastels—pink, yellow, and green—"you'll need a flower accent, too."

"Your mom is so cool," EJ whispered to Macy.

Macy grinned.

The girls had already enjoyed pizza and pop (EJ was disappointed to find out she could only eat two and a half pieces before she was too stuffed to eat more). After manis and pedis the three would retreat to the basement rec room to enjoy cookies and a DVD of *Anne of Green Gables* on a big-screen TV with surround sound.

"I'm really looking forward to watching this movie with you girls." Mrs. Russell turned off the drying fan and checked to make sure Macy's nails were set. "Macy keeps talking about how much she loves the book."

"Mom, it's seriously the best," Macy said. "You *have* to read it."

" 'Seriously the best'?" Mrs. Russell smiled. "That settles it. I'm definitely reading it."

"Mrs. Russell, I found my twenty reds." Macy motioned to the long row of bottles on the table in front of her. "What do we do first?"

"You could help me shake the bottles to make sure the paint hasn't separated." Mrs. Russell picked up a bottle by the cap and tapped it against the palm of her other hand. "Some of these might be a little old, so we'll need to check them."

"Sure, no problem." EJ snatched up the glossy red, but in the split second she lifted it from the table, she remembered she'd just set the lid on that one instead of screwing it on tightly. The round glass bottle fell away from the brush and spilled a glob of polish on the table.

"Oops!" Mrs. Russell swooped around the table, set right the bottle, and grabbed the cap from EJ in one fluid motion. "Just sit still and let me get a rag to get the worst of it, EJ."

"I'm sorry, Mrs. Russell." EJ felt an embarrassed lump form in her throat. "I'm just like Anne Shirley sometimes. Well-meaning but accident-prone."

"It's okay, hon. Anne sounds like she has a lot in common with all of us." Mrs. Russell's wet cloth wiped the excess paint from the tabletop, but an ugly red stain remained.

"Oh, man," EJ moaned. "I *ruined* your table!" EJ tried to calculate how many hours she'd have to babysit to make enough money to pay for a new table. Except she didn't know how much a table cost. Or the going rate for a babysitter, for that matter. So she estimated she might be able to pay off her debt by the time she turned twenty-eight.

"No, no, it's not ruined." Mrs. Russell produced a large bottle of fingernail polish remover and carefully used the stinky stuff to scrub the spot. In a matter of seconds, the tabletop looked good as new. "See?"

EJ breathed a sigh of relief.

"I think I'll let you take care of shaking the bottles," EJ said. "And I'll set up the pedicure station, okay, Mrs. Russell?"

"Good plan," Mrs. Russell said.

It was just after 11:30 p.m. as the closing credits for *Anne of Green Gables* scrolled on the TV, and even though Mrs. Russell said it was time for bed, Macy negotiated a midnight lights-out agreement with her mom. They just had to go to her room and not be too loud between now and then because Mrs. Russell said she was "too old to stay up past midnight" or she'd be "paying for it the next day."

EJ wondered what there was to regret about staying up past

midnight. As far as she was concerned, staying up late just meant she was having a good time. Now, being rudely woken up in the middle of the night by a screaming baby sister, *that* was something entirely different.

"Sweet dreams, girls." Mrs. Russell gave them each a kiss on the top of the head before she turned to leave Macy's bedroom.

"Night, Mom," Macy said.

"G'night, Mrs. Russell." EJ twinkled her fingers and wiggled her toes. "Thanks for doing my nails. They look *mah-velous.*"

"You're welcome, EJ. Good night." Mrs. Russell closed the bedroom door softly.

EJ squirmed excitedly in her sleeping bag on the air mattress next to Macy's daybed. "I'm not tired *at all,*" she said. "Are we *sure* that pop didn't have any caffeine in it?"

"I don't think orange soda has caffeine in it," Macy said. "But I'm not tired either. I don't think I could lie still and close my eyes even if I tried."

"What should we do?" EJ looked around the room for something fun—but quiet—they could do so they wouldn't wake up Mrs. Russell. She felt like she might already be on thin ice for spilling the nail polish, so she didn't want to do anything else that might result in never being invited back.

Macy snapped her fingers. "Bryan's star projector."

"What's a star projector?" EJ loved stars, so she was pretty sure she would like whatever this was.

"It's this thing Bryan got for Christmas that lights up and projects the image of the solar system on the ceiling," Macy explained. "And we can find constellations, too."

"It'll be like Camp Christian when we slept in the tent at

wilderness camp!" EJ smiled, remembering the week of church camp she spent with Macy the previous summer.

"The only thing is, we have to get it from Bryan's room." Macy bit her lip nervously. "And Mom said we're supposed to stay in my room."

"Well, *technically*"—EJ knew she was walking a fine line here, but that star projector sounded so cool—"she said we were supposed to 'go to' your room. She never said 'stay in.' "

Macy was unconvinced but seemed open to being talked into the idea.

"So as long as we're *quiet*," EJ continued. "We'll be fine."

Macy processed EJ's words a moment too long, and EJ figured she'd say no.

"Okay."

"Really?" EJ was honestly shocked that her rule-following best friend agreed to her suggestion.

"Yeah, I mean, if one of us had to go to the bathroom, Mom would obviously say it was okay to leave my bedroom." Macy's argument sounded logical to EJ. "So if we're quiet, we'll be fine."

A few minutes later, the beam of Macy's tiny flashlight sliced through the darkness of Bryan's room, hovering for a moment on his empty bed, then to his desk, and finally to the floor in the middle of the room. Macy led, with EJ right behind her, a hand on Macy's shoulder.

"Don't let go," Macy whispered. "Bryan's room isn't exactly clean, so there's a lot of stuff to trip over if you don't know what's in here."

"Why does it smell like a locker room?" EJ whispered, pinching her nose with her free hand.

"Teenage boys smell like sweat all the time," Macy said matter-of-factly. "One of the many reasons why Bryan is disgusting."

Oh, great, EJ thought. *Isaac will get grosser as he gets older.*

"There's the star projector." Macy pointed her flashlight at an object sitting on the floor a few feet away that looked a lot like a camping lantern.

"Rrrrrrrrrrrrrrr." A deep, rumbling growl comes from the corner of the darkened room. Macy and EJ freeze.

"Mace, did you adopt a giant dog I don't know about?"

"Not that I know of."

Grrrrrrrrrrrrrrrrr-snort-rrrrrrrrr.

EJ's imagination leaps from a snoozing furry pet to a vicious, rabid coyote. Or mountain lion. Or wolf. Yes, it's definitely a wolf. Are wolves native to Spooner? And if yes, how did one get into the Russells' house? And why is EJ wondering such things at a time like this?

"Macy, we're going to have to distract it to trap it," EJ whispers. "Otherwise, the wolf could attack us in our sleep—or worse, attack your mom."

Macy shines her flashlight on the floor around them, and they see mostly dirty, crumpled clothes and a few stuffed animals that look like they'd been well-loved for many years. Not the best weapons against a deadly beast. But still. . .

"Grrrrrrrrrrrroooooowwwwwwwl." The creature stirs and rises from the floor on its hind legs to its full height, silhouetted by the moon shining through the window behind it.

"Now!" The girls grab handfuls of clothes and toys and hurl them at the obviously bloodthirsty beast. Macy accidentally nudges the star projector with her foot and it falls over, turning on and splitting open to shine a spotlight-sized beam of light on the wolf. . . .

A skinny teenager, dressed in nothing but Spider-Man boxer shorts and a comforter around his shoulders, was blinded and dazed by the bright light shining straight in his eyes and the dirty clothes attacking him.

EJ gave a little squeak and covered her mouth with a hand to keep a threatening scream from coming out.

"Wha—? Whogoesdere?" Squinting and more than half asleep, Bryan Russell tripped on his comforter, flailed, and flopped down on his bed, where he immediately curled up into a ball and started snoring again.

"EJ, are you okay?"

"My heart's finally slowing down a bit," EJ whispered. Macy tiptoed to Bryan and arranged his comforter so he was covered up. EJ kept her distance, already a little weirded out that she had seen him in his boxer shorts.

"I thought you said Bryan was staying at a friend's house," EJ whispered. "And why was he sleeping on the floor?"

"He's a sleepwalker, and lots of times he wakes up in places in the house other than his bed," Macy said as she turned off the star projector and handed it to EJ. "He doesn't like spending the night at friends' houses because he never knows if he'll stay where he is supposed to. So I'm not really surprised he came home."

"Let's get outta here and back to your room," EJ said. "I don't think I'll ever be able to look at Spider-Man the same again."

Chapter 8

WEDDING PLANS

Dear Diary,

Since January, I've been taking lessons from the worship minister at our church. His name is Dane, and he is totally awesomesauce. He graduated from college a couple of years ago, so he's still young enough to not be entirely old and lame. He plays the guitar. And the bass guitar. And the piano. And the drums. And the harmonica. (Unfortunately, not all at the same time.) And now he's learning the ukulele and teaching me along the way. Basically, Diary, he loves music. And he's funny and nice, and I think he's very handsome (don't tell anyone). Usually if I think a boy is good-looking (like Cory Liden and his dimples), I'll describe him as *cute*. But Dane definitely qualifies as *handsome*. Well, handsome under the hot mess of a beard on his face right now. Several months ago, Dane started growing a beard. But it's not just any beard. According to Dad, Dane said he's trying to grow a yearlong beard—also known as a "yeard."

Sometimes Mom and Dad tease Dane about being Vine Street Community Church's "homeless worship dude," and they just laugh and shake their heads. I don't know much about shaving, Diary, but not shaving for a year seems sort of like something a crazy person would do. But if Dane is crazy, at least he's a crazy person with a goal.

After my ukulele lesson, Mrs. Winkle, Mom, and I are going shopping for some wedding inspiration. You know how I feel about shopping, Diary, but this sort of shopping seems completely different from grocery shopping (snooze!) or clothes shopping (double snooze!). Or maybe it has to do with the fact that my favoritest person, Mrs. Winkle, will be there. Honestly, Diary, *everything* is better with Mrs. Winkle.

EJ

EJ's fingers felt like Jell-O on the ukulele strings as she started and stopped her way through a verse of "Oh My Darling, Clementine."

"Rats!" EJ squeezed the uke by the neck to silence the strings that just weren't cooperating. "I'm never going to get this one."

"Come on, sure you will. Learning new music takes time." Dane stroked his beard in a way that reminded EJ of a mountain man. "Let's try playing it together."

"No! I want to do it myself!" EJ was getting flustered. "I *have* to do it myself if I'm going to play and sing at Mrs. Winkle's wedding."

"Hold on a second, EJ." Dane set his uke on his lap as the two sat on the steps on the stage of Vine Street Community Church. "After some practice, you'll get to the point where you can do it yourself, but you've got to let other people help you sometimes."

"But it's so easy for you!" EJ waved the ukulele by the neck, exasperated. "It's like you can pick up any instrument and just *know* how to play it. I wanna do that."

"It's not quite that simple, EJ," Dane said. "Anything worth doing is worth the work. Why is it that you want to play the ukulele, anyway?"

"I just thought being able to play the uke would be cooler than playing the piano or the clarinet like other kids my age," EJ said, adding silently to herself, *And if I wow people with my fantastic musical talents, all the better.*

"You like to be special—to stick out in a crowd. That's cool, EJ." Dane tapped the hollow body of his ukulele with his fingertips. "But sometimes you have to admit that you need help to get there."

EJ raised an eyebrow, confused. "If I know I can do it, why wouldn't I just work hard and figure it out myself?"

"Well, one reason is that your friends—like me—*want* to help you. Just the same way that I know you like to help other people." Dane pulled a phone out of his pocket and tapped the screen. "And a second reason is that God is glorified when we accept help from others."

EJ thought that might be the weirdest thing she'd ever heard. Maybe Dane's beard was growing into his brain.

"Sometimes when I'm trying to do everything myself or if I'm working on a new piece of music and it's not as easy as I thought it'd be, I remind myself of what the Bible says in Ecclesiastes 4:9–10." Dane held out his phone to EJ so she could read from the screen.

" 'Two people are better off than one, for they can help each other succeed. If one person falls, the other can reach out and help. But someone who falls alone is in real trouble.' "

"When we accept help from others, we're honoring God because it helps make us humble and less focused on ourselves," Dane said. "And then, with God at the center of everything we do, the pressure is off us to be perfect. You can be confident and know that God'll help you do your very best for His glory."

EJ absentmindedly strummed a C chord. She thought she still would like to just do things herself—when she could.

"Do you think you can *help* me learn 'You Are My Sunshine'?" EJ looked hopefully at Dane. "Mrs. Winkle's wedding is just a few weeks away, and I want to make sure I know it really well."

"Two of my favorites: Mrs. Winkle and 'You Are My Sunshine,' " Dane said, smiling. "Let's work through it together."

The crystal-clear ocean water gently laps the white sandy beach as the

tropical breeze tickles palm tree leaves high above. The groom fidgets nervously in his Hawaiian shirt and khaki cargo shorts, his ghost white legs mostly covered by long black socks and sandals on his feet. (EJ shakes her head and smiles to herself, amused by Mr. Johnson's lack of fashion sense.) The white-haired man stands in the sand under an arch adorned with green palm fronds and hot pink exotic flowers. His entire face lights up and he stands a little taller, and EJ knows the time is almost here.

EJ looks across the tops of the heads of the wedding guests to see the lovely bride take her place at the edge of the sand. She strums the first few chords of the simple but beautiful tune and inhales the salty sea air into her lungs before singing in her clear soprano voice, "You are my sunshine. . . ."

"I'd love to have a Hawaiian destination wedding." Mrs. Winkle sighed and untied the vintage grass skirt that had triggered EJ's daydream. "If only Honolulu weren't four-thousand twenty-eight miles away from Spooner."

"That's a very specific number of miles, Wilma," Mom said, taking the grass skirt from Mrs. Winkle and hanging it on a display of authentic Hawaiian clothes.

"I Googled the distance from Spooner to Honolulu." Mrs. Winkle's eyes twinkled. "A girl can dream."

"I know you'll come up with a fabulous plan for your wedding, Mrs. Winkle." EJ returned a flower lei to the display and glanced around the antique shop full of interesting goods for sale. "I mean, you're the most creative person I know."

"The child speaks truth!" Miss Adele, the shopkeeper of Miss Adele's Antiquities, popped out from behind a display of mismatched trophies, some of them more than seventy years old but shining like they were brand new. "I gave up any hope I had to be as creative as you years ago, Wilma."

Miss Adele was a feisty little lady, a retired junior high algebra teacher, and one of Mrs. Winkle's good friends from the bowling league. Miss Adele loved helping people plan their events, and even though she wouldn't admit it, Miss Adele had almost as many fascinating ideas as Mrs. Winkle. The shopkeeper wore multiple layers of sparkly, gauzy shawls on her thin shoulders and more jingly bangles on her wrists than EJ could count. The reading glasses propped on her head were encrusted with multicolored jewels, only matched by the large rings on nearly every finger. Miss Adele greeted Mrs. Winkle, Mom, and EJ with an air kiss on each cheek—"like the Europeans do," she'd explained the first time EJ and she met.

"Adele, I should've come to you weeks ago—I don't know where to begin with this wedding business!" Mrs. Winkle held her face in her hands as she looked around the store. "Classic and serious or fun and frivolous?"

"Oh dear, I'd hate to think those were our only two options!" Mrs. Winkle, Mom, and EJ followed Miss Adele as she weaved through the merchandise until she stopped in front of a display of vintage cowboy boots and hats. "How about an Old West wedding?"

"Ya'll, we're gathered here today to celebrate the hitchin' of this here cowpoke to this here cowgirl." The spurs on Dad's boot clink as he kicks away a tumbleweed blowing toward the wedding decorations.

The wind kicks up across the prairie, and EJ pulls her neckerchief to cover her nose and mouth. The leather fringe on Mrs. Winkle's wedding dress dances in the breeze, and a sudden gust of dust blows Mr. Johnson's hat sky-high.

"Too windy." Mrs. Winkle brushed her hand along the brim of a cowboy hat. "And think of the dust!"

"What about a Classic Hollywood theme?" EJ pointed to an old-timey reel-to-reel movie projector.

The Big Band music fills the auditorium as the bride starts her confident stroll down the red carpet lining the aisle. Mrs. Winkle is bathed in the halo of a spotlight that follows her every move. A single red rose tucked behind her ear completes the elegant beauty of her simple white dress and long white gloves. Standing at the altar, Mr. Johnson's black tuxedo with tails is only perfected by a classic black bow tie and top hat. The lights go down as a click and whirr of a flickering movie projector means the love story of the bride and groom is about to begin.

"Lester would never go for it. He despises movies." Mrs. Winkle chuckled. "He told me that ever since he saw *Old Yeller* in the theater and cried like a baby at the end, he swore he'd never go see another movie and risk crying in public." Mrs. Winkle covered her mouth with her hand, and her eyes got wide. "I probably shouldn't have told you that."

"We'll keep it a secret, won't we, EJ?" Mom smiled.

EJ thought it was kind of nice that grisly old Mr. Johnson was sensitive enough that he'd cried in a movie where a boy had to say good-bye to his pet. "His secret is safe with me," EJ said.

"You know what Lester would really like?" Mrs. Winkle asked no one in particular. "An elopement."

Mr. Johnson looks perfectly at ease in the Spooner city courthouse—on a Tuesday morning. He leans against his cane, wearing his everyday clothes of a button-down plaid shirt and slacks. Mrs. Winkle, carrying a bouquet of white daisies and wearing a simple cotton dress with tiny wedding cakes all over it, hooks her arm onto his as they walk a few steps to stand before the judge.

"Not an option!" Miss Adele busted into EJ's daydream. "You're not getting married in the courthouse, Wilma!"

Just then, Mom's phone rang.

"Hi, honey." By Mom's tone, EJ knew Dad was the "honey" on the other end of the line. "Oh my goodness, that's hilarious. Yeah, hold on, let me put you on speakerphone." Mom tapped the phone's screen. "Okay, David, you're on speaker."

"Big news!" Dad's voice sounded breathless and excited. "We have a walker!"

A week ago, Faith had taken her first wobbly steps across the living room and since then had been right on the verge of becoming a full-fledged walking machine. She had been trying so hard to master the skill, and EJ could see her own frustration in her sister's face every time she fell on her diapered behind.

Bert's distressed bark sounded in the background of the phone call.

"Is Bert okay?" EJ strained to hear more from him on the phone. "He sounds like he's trapped in a cave."

"That's the funny part of all of this." Dad chuckled. "Faith's first real steps weren't so much walking as they were *running*. And she *sprinted* after Bert."

"Oh dear." Mrs. Winkle grinned. "What did our furry friend do?"

"Well, he ran as fast as he could from her," Dad said. "And when I caught up with the two of them, Faith had cornered him here in the mudroom, and he is currently peeking his head out of the opening of the empty clothes dryer! She giggled and laughed and was so proud of herself. Poor ol' Bertie's life just got a whole lot more interesting."

Everyone laughed.

EJ felt bad for Bert, but she had to admit that the scene happening at home sounded pretty stinking funny. "This must be Faith's way of getting back at Bert for destroying her favorite pacifiers," EJ said.

EJ had always been proud of the fact that she had a better-than-average vocabulary. But as she read the caterer's menu on the card in front of her, she thought maybe she didn't know very many words after all:

HORS D'OEUVRE
MINIATURE TORTILLA CUPS
WITH CHIPOTLE GLAZED ROCK SHRIMP

FIRST COURSE
CHILLED SPRING GAZPACHO

ENTRÉE
ROASTED FILET MIGNON
POTATO GALETTE, SAUTÉED SPINACH, ROASTED MUSHROOM

"These samples are all delicious, but it's too fancy for my taste," Mrs. Winkle whispered to Mom and EJ as Cady of Cady's Catering hurried to clear the dishes from the table. "And Lester told me he'd like it if we just served cold cuts on a tray at the reception."

Mom laughed. "Lester is a man of simple tastes."

"The word you're looking for is *cheap*, dear." Mrs. Winkle

smiled. "But I might just agree with him in this instance." EJ could see that Mrs. Winkle's creative mind was trying to come up with a way to make lunch meat work elegantly at a wedding reception.

"Soooo, bride-to-be, how much do you *love* the menu I've selected especially for you?" the caterer gushed, her large, white teeth gleaming from her big smile. "It's to *die* for, right?"

"The menu certainly is. . .impressive." Mrs. Winkle chose her words carefully. "But I will need some time to think about the options and talk to the groom-to-be."

"Sure! Sure, no problem!" A pink lipstick smudge appeared on Cady's front teeth. EJ subconsciously ran her tongue over her teeth. "Are we ready for the cake test, ladies?"

Yes! The cake! This was the part of today's wedding shopping trip that EJ had been waiting for! Cake, in EJ's humble opinion, was the very best wedding tradition of them all. White cake, chocolate cake, marble, strawberry-filled, angel food, pound cake—EJ thought there was something almost magical about the way wedding cakes tasted.

"Ta-da!" Cady removed a silver dome from a cake stand to reveal a masterpiece of confection perfection: a four-tiered square cake, perfectly smooth fondant, the crease of each layer lined with tiny white pearls. But the best part was an explosion of vibrantly colored flowers that cascaded over the top of the cake and draped beautifully down the side.

"Oh, how lovely." EJ realized her mouth was hanging open in amazement, so she shut it quickly. "How did you get the red frosting for the flowers so *red*? My red frosting always ends up pink, no matter how much red food coloring I put in it."

"It's a secret I only tell my best clients." Cady smiled at EJ.

"They're made of a special sugar—not frosting and food coloring."

"It's perfect—exactly what I am looking for," Mrs. Winkle said. "Now if it tastes half as good as it looks, you've got yourself an order, Cady."

The caterer cut three pieces from the top layer and set them on plates. EJ was disappointed that none of the slices included sugar flowers. She really wanted to try one.

Realizing she'd left the forks in the kitchen, Cady left the room and promised to be right back, and Mom and Mrs. Winkle scooted their chairs together to look at the caterer's album full of pictures of past cakes. EJ felt her fingers itch as she looked longingly at the sugar flowers. Surely she could take one from the cake and nobody would miss it. She glanced at Mom and Mrs. Winkle, who were oohing and aahing over a groom's cake that looked like a classic car— something Mr. Johnson, a retired used-car salesman, would love.

Before EJ realized she'd plucked it, she had an intricately beautiful red sugar rose in her hand.

"Here we are—dessert forks!" EJ panicked at Cady's sudden appearance and she tossed the flower in her mouth to get rid of the evidence. "Enjoy!"

Mom and Mrs. Winkle dug into their cake samples and immediately began raving about the dessert's "perfect texture" and "just right amount of sweetness" and "divine flavor."

"Aren't you going to try it, sweetie?" Mom peered at EJ. "I thought you were looking forward to the cake testing."

"Imnohungee." EJ's attempt to talk around the sugar flower was a failure.

"Are you okay, EJ?" Mrs. Winkle looked concerned. "Your speech is garbled."

EJ had a choice to make: spit out the flower and deal with the consequences of taking it without asking or. . . .

Crunch, crunch. The sugar flower was so rock-hard that EJ thought that must be what it would be like to chew on gravel. *Just chew a few more times and you'll be able to swallow it,* EJ coached herself.

Crunch, crunch, CRACK! The sound vibrated in EJ's head. But what caused it? Finally, mercifully, she was able to swallow the flower.

Cady's eyes grew as she pointed to the spot where the rose was missing. "EJ, did you *eat* one of the flowers?"

EJ couldn't think of a way out of this one, so she nodded. "Yesh." Yesh? What was that? "I'm shorry, it jusht looked sho nishe." Why was she talking like a weirdo?

"Emma Jean Payne!" Mom meant business, but her eyes had a mix of surprise, horror, and. . .amusement? "You chipped a tooth on a stolen sugar flower!"

A chipped tooth! Immediately her tongue found the problem—part of her front tooth was gone! Her hand flew to cover her mouth. Why hadn't she just admitted she took it?

"EJ, those flowers are made of sugar, but you're not really supposed to eat them!" Cady looked horrified. "This is my fault. I should've warned you."

"Oh, EJ, only you." Mom smiled weakly. "Guess it's time to call the dentist."

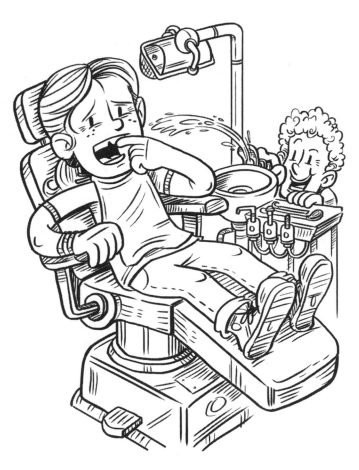

Chapter 9

WHISTLER'S BROTHER

Dear Diary,

This chipped tooth is pretty much the most embarrassing thing ever. Not only do I look completely silly, but every s out of my mouth comes with a high-pitched whistle. I've tried whispering. I've tried talking with my lips curled around my teeth (making me look like a toothless old lady). I've even tried speaking out of the side of my mouth, but the only remedy for keeping my chipped-tooth whistle silent is not to talk.

Not talking is *nearly* impossible for me, Diary. So when Mom called our dentist, Dr. Molnar, to make an appointment to get my tooth fixed, I was relieved to hear they had an opening first thing Monday morning. In fact, I was so happy I didn't have to whistle my way through school that I didn't mind (much) that Isaac is going along for a teeth cleaning, too.

I loved going to the dentist when I was little, Diary. They give you bubblegum-flavored fluoride, your very own pack of sugar-fee gum, a brand-new toothbrush and floss, and a sticker with a smiling cartoon tooth. But then you turn seven, develop a love for gummy bears, and forget to brush your teeth once too often, get your first cavity, and WHAMMO! The medieval torture tools come out! After experiencing the drill, I can't even imagine what kinds of crazy tools Dr. Molnar will use to fix a busted tooth like mine.

Last night I had a dream that I went to the dentist and Dr. Molnar pulled out all my teeth and gave me a set of dentures to wear! When I woke up, all my teeth felt loose until I wiggled each one and confirmed they were all still solidly attached to my gums. Dad assures me that the dentist will fix my tooth and not just pull it out and make me wear a fake one. I hope he's right, Diary. Mr. Johnson wears dentures, and I love the guy, but his teeth sometimes look like Chiclets—you know, those square pieces of white gum that you can buy at the grocery store checkout?

EJ

"Hey, EJ." Isaac twisted in his car seat toward his sister. "Guess what."

EJ lifted her hands palms up and shrugged her shoulders in a wordless, "What?"

"No, you have to guess!" EJ knew Isaac just wanted her to talk so he could hear her tooth whistle, but she wasn't planning to make another peep until her tooth was fixed, if she could help it. EJ made the zipped-lip motion across her mouth, locked it with an imaginary key, and pretended to throw it out of the minivan window.

"Oh, you're no fun." Isaac crossed his arms and faced the front of the minivan as Dad drove them through Spooner to the dentist office on the other side of town. "If I had a sweet whistle like yours, I'd learn how to whistle a tune with it. And I'd say as many *s* words as I could. I would read the *s* section from the dictionary! From the encyclopedia! From Wikipedia!"

Dad flipped the turn signal and turned right at a stop sign. "Isaac, did you brush your teeth before we left the house?"

"Why would I brush my teeth?" Isaac looked at Dad like he was crazy. "That's what I'm going to the dentist for, right? *He's* going to clean my teeth."

"Ishaac!" EJ couldn't stay silent, whistling tooth or not. "You can't go to the dentisht with dirty teeth and dishgushting bad breath! What will Dr. Molnar think?"

"Dr. Molnar will be laughing so hard at my dentist joke that he won't even notice my dirty teeth," Isaac said. "Dad, I've got a joke for you. What time is a dentist's favorite time?"

Another new joke? Isaac was really branching out in his comedy.

"I give up," Dad said, glancing in the rearview mirror at his son.

"Tooth hurty." Isaac laughed like it was the funniest thing he'd ever heard in his life. Dad chuckled and shook his head. EJ just rolled her eyes. "Get it, EJ? Two thirty—tooth hurty?"

Back to the not-talking thing, EJ gave Isaac a thumbs-up and a sarcastic smile. She couldn't wait to get this dentist appointment over with so she could go to school and have a few hours away from the Space Invader.

EJ sat partially reclined in the dental chair. She felt her heart beating faster than normal and tried to calm her nerves by taking deep, even breaths. She closed her eyes and willed herself to start a daydream.

But all she saw was the back of her eyelids. Why was it that she could easily slip into her imagination when she wasn't supposed to, but when she really could use a daydream, she couldn't start one? She opened her eyes and looked around the exam area for some inspiration: a box of latex gloves, a glass jar of cotton squares, a tray laid with dental instruments. Nothing looked remotely interesting until an oil painting on the wall caught her attention—a beautiful landscape of a calm body of water that reminded her of the lake at Camp Christian. . . .

The morning sun's first rays spill over the horizon as EJ paddles her kayak to the middle of the peaceful lake. The blades of her oar make tiny circular ripples each time she dips an end into the water and pulls the water past her. Her sleek kayak moves easily through the still water. In the distance, a bird chirps a happy morning tune and water bugs flit across the glassy surface of the lake.

EJ leans back against the kayak's seat and fills her lungs with the crisp morning air. Calm, serene. . .wet!

A spray of water hits EJ square in the face.

"Bulls-eye!"

Sputtering and wiping the water away with her T-shirt sleeve, EJ sat bolt upright in the chair, rudely yanked from her short daydream distraction.

"Ishaac!" EJ had almost forgotten about her broken-tooth whistle. "Get losht!"

Isaac gripped the dental water sprayer in his hand like a gun, aiming right at EJ. "Reach for the sky," Isaac said, using his best cowboy drawl. "I'm the sheriff in these here parts, and we don't take kindly to no daydreamin'."

EJ lunged to grab the sprayer, but Isaac pulled it out of her reach and set it back in its holder, turning just in time to put on his very best innocent face as Dr. Molnar entered the exam room.

"Ah, I see my assistant is here already," the short, bald, smiley dentist said. Isaac was the only other person in the room other than EJ. Surely Dr. Molnar didn't mean. . . . "Ready to get started, Isaac?"

"I think you're going to be extremely happy with the results of our work, Miss Payne." Isaac, dressed in blue scrubs, glances up at EJ from the clipboard in his hand. "My assistance to Dr. Molnar was very helpful."

EJ holds up a hand mirror and smiles widely to survey the results of the dental procedure. She gasps and immediately clamps her mouth shut at the sight of her teeth.

"I suggested that we could improve your teeth by sharpening each one to a razor-edged point, just like the teeth of a T-Rex," Isaac says. "And Dr. Molnar said that was the very best idea he'd ever heard in his life."

"But I don't want T-Rex teeth!"

"Whoshe idea wash it to make Ishaac the dental asshishtant?" EJ demanded, glaring at Isaac. "Why aren't you in the waiting room with Dad?"

"Don't worry, EJ, I'm still in charge," Dr. Molnar said, trying to hide a smile at EJ's tooth whistle. "Your dad had a couple of errands to run, and Isaac has certain skills that I think will come in handy in the procedure today." EJ found that very hard to believe. "Isaac, here's the book you'll need." Isaac took the small paperback from Dr. Molnar and sat on the foot of EJ's dental chair, grinning at her.

EJ gave Isaac a look that said, "You'd better not mess this up, kid" and nervously bit the corner of her mouth as Dr. Molnar snapped on a pair of gloves and a mask and readied the items on the tray.

"All right, EJ." Even though EJ couldn't see Dr. Molnar's mouth behind the mask, she could tell by his eyes that he was still smiling. "Open wide."

EJ opened her mouth and winced a bit as she heard the unmistakable *zizzzz* of a dental instrument. This one sounded different than the piercing sound of a high-speed cavity drill. No, it sounded lower—more like a grinder.

"It's not going to hurt; it'll just feel a little strange," Dr. Molnar assured her, but she gripped the chair's armrests all the same. EJ's eyes went a little crossed as she watched the dentist bring the small, rotating disc toward her broken tooth.

Dear God, EJ fervently prayed, *please let this not hurt. I'm sorry I took the sugar flower without asking, and I promise I'll never take anything that isn't mine again, and I'm definitely* not *putting anything in my mouth without finding out if it's safe to eat first!*

Zizzzzzzgggggrrrrr. Dr. Molnar hummed a nameless song as the grinder made contact with EJ's tooth. She dug her fingernails straight into the chair's armrest, wondering if she was actually making holes in the plastic covering.

"Hey, EJ." EJ's eyes darted toward her feet, where she had almost forgotten Isaac sat. Up on his knees, he held open the book titled *101 Punny Jokes for Dentists.* "What do you call a dentist who doesn't like tea?"

EJ's eyes shifted to Dr. Molnar, expecting him to tell Isaac to sit down and behave (or maybe even to go out into the waiting room), but instead the dentist kept intently working on EJ's tooth and said simply, "Oh, that's a good one. EJ, you'll like this one."

What kind of a weird upside-down world was this that Dr. Molnar's "assistant" was a six-year-old spaz whose main purpose was to distract the dentist with corny jokes?

"EJ, do you know the answer?" Isaac sat up taller on his knees so he was sure EJ could see him. "What do you call a dentist who doesn't like tea?"

"Ionknow." EJ shrugged, giving up trying to figure out what was really going on.

"Denis!" Isaac laughed and rolled off the end of the chair and onto the floor, overcome by the hilarity of the joke. Dr. Molnar returned the grinder to its spot on the tray and sat back in his chair as he belly-laughed. After several seconds, Isaac caught his breath and said, "Do you get it, EJ? Denis is *dentist* without *t*!"

"Hilarioush." EJ did enjoy a good spelling joke now and then, but she didn't feel like laughing.

"There now, EJ, you've made it through the toughest part of

the tooth restoration." Dr. Molnar pulled the mask away from his mouth so he could talk easier. "Isaac, you did a fantastic job keeping your sister's mind off of what was happening."

So *that's* what was going on. Even though EJ felt a little tricked, she had to admit that Isaac's distraction had worked pretty well.

"Do I get a paycheck for my fantastic job as your assistant?" Isaac's face was hopeful.

"How about I give you a checkup and a teeth cleaning?" Dr. Molnar counter-offered. "And then your dad can pay for it."

"Will you throw in a big, round sticker with a cartoon tooth on it?" Isaac was playing hardball.

"Deal." Dr. Molnar and Isaac shook on it.

A half hour later, EJ's tooth was completely restored to its pre-chipped glory. (EJ even thought the new part of the tooth might be a little straighter than the old one.) She sat in a plastic chair in the corner of the room reading a book about dental history, and Isaac was in the reclining chair, Dr. Molnar giving him a checkup.

"Whoa, Dr. Molnar, it says here that in the 1800s, some barbers were the first dentists in the Old West." EJ held up the book to show the illustration. "A customer would come in with tooth pain, and the barber would pull a tooth for a small fee."

"And then talk him into getting a trim and a shave while he was already in the chair," Dr. Molnar said. "Isaac, can I interest you in a haircut?"

"No thank you, but I think I'm due for a shave." Isaac rubbed his chin the same way Dad did when he was whiskery.

EJ and Dr. Molnar laughed, and the dentist swiveled in his chair to review Isaac's dental X-ray. EJ returned to her book.

"Hey, Isaac-man, I've got a joke for you," Dr. Molnar said a minute later, jotting a note on Isaac's patient file. "What did the dentist say to the golfer?"

"Oh! I remember that one from the book," Isaac said. "He said, 'You have a hole in one!' "

Isaac erupted in laughter, and EJ chuckled. Dr. Molnar smiled, but he looked a little sad at the same time.

"Isaac, you have a hole in one." Isaac stopped laughing and looked at the dentist. "You have your first cavity."

Isaac's eyes got wide, and he took a deep breath. "So what you're saying is that you're going to have to pull all of my teeth, right?"

"No, Isaac, this isn't 1832!" EJ was amazed at her brother's ignorance. "Dr. Molnar will fix it with a filling!"

Isaac visibly relaxed with this news.

"Normally you'd need to come back again for another appointment, but I have an opening, so we can take care of this right now," Dr. Molnar said. "Are you ready, Isaac?"

Isaac nodded, and the dentist pushed a pedal on the floor that made the chair recline all the way back.

Dr. Molnar placed a small rubber mask over Isaac's nose, hooked it to a tube that led to a canister under the counter, and instructed Isaac to breathe through his nose.

"You're breathing in nitrous oxide," Dr. Molnar explained. "This stuff is better for kids' cavities than Novocain shots. It takes a few minutes to start working, so I'll be back in just a bit. Make sure he stays there, breathing the laughing gas, EJ."

Dr. Molnar shut the door softly behind him.

"Did he say *laughing* gas?" The mask made Isaac sound a little like he was pinching his nose when he talked. "Is this going to be like Uncle Albert on *Mary Poppins*? This stuff makes me laugh and then I float up into the air?"

EJ secretly wished that were the case. "I don't think so, Isaac." Isaac closed his eyes and concentrated on breathing through his nose. A minute later, his eyelids fluttered open slightly, and he looked sidelong at EJ through half-closed lids.

"Hey, EJ, remember at family camp when we pretended that I was a dolphin and you were a dolphin trainer?" Isaac didn't stop to let EJ reply. "Or the time that you cut the bald spot on my head? Hey, remember when we shoveled snow off of Mr. Johnson's driveway with Dad—when we were still really afraid of him? Oh, and that time that you were the Christmas angel and got to be in the harness and fly in the pageant? Man, that was so cool." Isaac slumped back in the chair, and EJ could tell that the nitrous oxide was starting to take effect.

"Yeah, those are pretty great memories, Isaac." EJ set the book aside and scooted her chair closer to Isaac's, wondering what he'd say next.

"Oh! EJ! Code Christmas, when we gave Christmas to the McCallisters in secret!" Isaac looked around the room to make sure nobody was listening, and continued, whispering, "That was the best night ever. You know what, EJ? You have the best ideas."

"Thanks." Isaac had never really said such nice things about EJ before. It must've been the laughing gas talking, right?

"And remember last summer during the swing set switcharoo, we built the tree house? And remember when we pretended to break out of jail? And then we went to camp together." Isaac giggled. "And *that* was the best day ever—when I got to go to camp with you."

EJ was going to correct Isaac that they didn't technically go to camp *together*. She was there all week, and he came for day camp. But he seemed to be having such a great time walking down memory lane that she decided to let his laughing-gassed brain remember what it wanted to remember.

"You know how you've been giving me Oreos, EJ? I love Oreos." Isaac smiled a loopy smile and mimed eating a pretend Oreo. "But those worms that we pretended you ate were almost as gross as the squash Mom tried to feed us. And—EW, GROSS!— Faith *liked* it!" Isaac was veering off the path of sanity and getting louder and sillier by the second. "Oohh, EJ—I feel like I'm floating! Awesomesauce!"

"It's just the laughing gas working, Isaac," EJ said. "I'm sure Dr. Molnar will be back any min—"

"Do you wanna hear a secret, EJ?" Isaac jutted a finger at her and his eyes crossed a tiny bit. "The secret is, I like to bug you, and I like being the Space Invader."

Isaac's eyes suddenly cleared, the loopiness gone for a moment. "But what I like the most is when we imagine adventures *together*, EJ." A goofy grin spread across his face, and he snorted a little chuckle—the laughing gas had taken a firm hold of his brain. "And I think you're way groovy to the max, dude."

EJ's chest felt warm and she smiled at her little brother as he lay back and started loudly counting the tiles on the ceiling, off in his own little world.

Chapter 10

Adventures in Babysitting

Dear Diary,

My infant home care professional certification is framed and on the wall in my bedroom. I have my *Babysitting 101* handbook ready, complete with my own notes in the margins and Post-its marking the most important pages. There's a list of emergency numbers posted on the wall next to the phone in the kitchen. I'm dressed in comfortable clothes (jeans and a well-worn Spooner Elementary School hoodie), my hair is pulled back into a ponytail, and I am not wearing any jewelry that a baby can yank and break. My hands are washed and dried, and I drank a bottle of water so I am well-hydrated and feeling fantastic.

Let's do this babysitting thing!

Mom has parent-teacher conferences (as the teacher, this time) for a couple of hours tonight, and Dad is leading a Bible study at church. So for the first time ever, I will be large and in charge at home as babysitter extraordinaire. Isaac wasn't too keen on the idea of me being his babysitter—"I'm six! I haven't been a baby for at least five years!" he said. (Side note: Isaac threw a temper tantrum last week when he couldn't get a knot out of his shoelace, so I personally think he might actually *still* be a baby.) Mom told Isaac he could be my assistant, but only if he accepted two Chips Ahoy cookies as payment. Isaac counter-offered by saying he would only accept Oreos. (Another side note: Mom doesn't know about the Oreo training, so the whole thing was a pretty funny coincidence.) When Isaac left the room, Mom told me in a low voice that was an innocent trick to make Isaac okay with the babysitting situation. And she said I might even get him to help me out by referring to him as my "assistant."

That Mom. She's pretty smart. (Obviously that's where I get it.)

I'd better go downstairs for last-minute instructions from Mom before she heads out the door. If I time this right, I might get her to change one more diaper before she leaves (aka one less diaper that I'll have to change).

I've got this babysitting thing in the bag.

EJ

"Okay, Faith, here are the plans for tonight." EJ paced in front of the crib and used her best I'm-in-charge voice. "First, your after-dinner nap."

Faith pressed her face through the crib bars like a prisoner yearning to get out of jail and watched EJ carefully.

"Then your bath, followed by some playtime. And finally, to bed." Faith blew some slobbery raspberries to let EJ know what she thought about those plans.

EJ pressed a button on her wristwatch. "Mom said you'd sleep for about an hour, so I'm starting the timer. Go to sleep. . .now."

"That's not how Marmalade does it." Isaac stood in the doorway. "She rocks Faith in the glider till she falls asleep."

"Oh, she does? Okay." EJ sized up Faith, who was now standing in the crib, peering at her big sister, grinning. She was a lot bigger than Abner, the infant simulator, so rocking Faith to sleep might be a challenge. "Thanks, Isaac."

"Your infant home care assistant, at your service." Isaac bowed. "If you need me, I'll be building a Lego castle in my room that will soon be invaded by dinosaurs and storm troopers in twenty minutes." Isaac spun around in a superhero-like move and streaked down the hallway.

Faith giggled and squealed excitedly at Isaac's dramatic exit.

"All right, girlie. Nap time." EJ lowered the light in the room with the dimmer on the wall and turned on a night-light that spun slowly, projecting images of colorful flowers on the wall. Faith's face lit up at the sight of the flowers—as if they were the best thing she'd ever seen. EJ smiled and picked Faith up from the crib, grunting a little in the process.

"I need to start lifting weights," EJ said, settling on the chair and pulling Faith on her lap. "You're a bowling ball that's too heavy for me."

"Ba-ba-ba," Faith echoed the sounds she heard from EJ's mouth.

"Yep, that's good, Faith." She leaned back in the glider and tried to hold Faith the way she'd seen Mom hold her while she slept. "B-b-ball."

Faith's feet hung off of EJ's lap, and her tiny fingers clutched onto handfuls of Spooner Elementary hoodie fabric. EJ's lap felt much too small, and Faith felt much too big. Forget about head and neck support; one wrong move by either of them and Faith could easily slip off. EJ was completely uncomfortable, and judging by the look on Faith's face, she was not only uncomfortable, but fearing for her life.

"All right then, Plan B." EJ stood and hoisted Faith back into her crib. Then she took her wristwatch off and swung it like a pendulum in front of Faith's face. "You're getting sleepy. Very, very sleepy." Faith's chubby hand grabbed the watch with a death grip and tried pulling it to her mouth.

"No! No! Yucky!" It took all of EJ's strength to pry Faith's surprisingly strong fingers from the watch.

Just then, Bert trotted into the room to see what all the commotion was about. A crazy idea flashed across EJ's mind—so crazy that it just might work.

"Hey, Bertie, you wanna help me with something, boy?" Bert wagged his tail. One of Faith's new favorite things to do was dress up her dolls in different clothes, so maybe. . .

A few minutes later, Bert was less than impressed with the outfit EJ had dressed him in. . .a diaper and one of Faith's flower headbands. "All you have to do is pretend to go to sleep," Faith explained to him. "She likes to imitate others, so maybe if Faith sees you go to sleep, she'll do the same thing."

Faith's dark eyes locked on the dressed-up Bert as he sighed and turned in three circles before lying down amid a herd of stuffed animals propped next to the changing table. For added believability, he started snoring. "Good job, Bert," EJ whispered. Then she realized he was *actually* asleep. Now if only Faith would fall asleep that easily.

EJ glanced back at the crib and saw that Faith was lying down as well, watching Bert through the bars of the crib. *Now, just close your eyes,* EJ silently pleaded with Faith. But a few seconds later, Faith must've realized that the Bert show was over because she rolled over and pushed herself up while letting loose with a "Baaaaaa–eeeeeeeee–iiiiiii–aaaaaaaah!" that sounded a little bit like a Tarzan yell.

Bert bolted up and gave a deep warning bark (EJ couldn't blame him—the sound Faith had just made was terrifying!). Bert's bark scared Faith, who immediately burst into tears.

"Shhh, shhh. It's okay." EJ picked up the crying Faith and tried to comfort her. Bert resumed his spot among the animals and watched them warily. "You scared Bert, and Bert scared you."

EJ handed Faith her favorite teething toy from the diaper bag next to the rocking chair, a squeezy giraffe that squeaked. Faith stopped crying and gnawed on the giraffe's neck, and EJ set her on the floor. She found a pack of mint gum in the diaper bag and popped a piece in her mouth. Chewing gum always helped her think.

Squeak. Squeak-squeak-squeak. Rocking didn't work. Hypnotism was a bust. Trying to get Faith to follow Bert's lead ended in tears. *Squeakity-squea-squea-SQUEAK!*

With Faith distracted by the squeaker toy, EJ turned to the "What to Do When Baby Won't Sleep" section in her *Babysitting 101* handbook sitting on top of the changing table. She read:

> *Nap time can be a big challenge for the babysitter. Without the normal rituals that a parent may provide, babies may have a difficult time falling asleep. Or, because they have someone new and different to interact with, babies may be more interested in playing than sleeping. A babysitter can use this to her advantage. Short bursts of high-energy play may be just the thing for tiring a baby for nap time.*

"Perfect!" EJ snapped her fingers. "Faith, how about a dance party?"

Squeeeeeeeeeeeak. EJ took that as a yes. She double-checked the floor where Faith was sitting to make sure there was nothing dangerous around her. "Be right back. Bert, you're in charge." Bert snorted. EJ sprinted next door to her room and grabbed her desktop stereo and mini MP3 player and was back rounding the doorway in less than eight seconds.

"What do we feel like? How about some oldie—" The scene in front of EJ made her stop short. Somehow—in just eight seconds—Faith had traveled the ten feet from where EJ had left her on the floor to the diaper bag and had opened an entire box of animal crackers and crushed them into crumbs and was now grinding them into the carpet with her hands. Faith giggled as Bert licked animal cracker dust off her left cheek.

"Never leave baby unattended." Miss Debbie's warning filled EJ's brain. Too late. The damage was already done.

"Ahh! Faith! Bert!" Faith glanced up from her delightfully fun animal cracker mess and grinned at EJ. Bert, realizing they were probably in trouble, took a few steps from Faith and sat on his diapered bottom, putting on his best it-was-the-baby's-idea face.

"Let's clean this up," EJ said. She couldn't help but be impressed with the speed at which Faith was able to make such a colossal mess as she used a wet wipe to clean Faith's hands and face and brush away the crumbs from her onesie. She slid Faith away from the crumbs and pulled the vacuum cleaner out of the closet. "Cleaning is always better after a little dancing, anyway." Leaving the vacuum standing in the middle of the room, EJ flipped through the songs on her MP3 player.

"Oh yeah, here's a good one." A few moments later, the bass line of the song "Twist and Shout" blared from the small speakers. Faith clapped excitedly as EJ picked her up and started twisting in time to the music. During the chorus, EJ set Faith on her feet on the floor. Faith's fingers curled around EJ's pointer fingers, and they both did the twist.

"Nice moves, Faith-girl!" Faith let go of EJ's fingers and wobbled for a second before expertly falling on her diaper-padded bottom. EJ took the opportunity to really amp up her moves and show Faith what a great dancer she was. EJ was getting into the dancing so much that she didn't realize when she bumped into the diaper bag, tipping it over. Faith babbled and giggled and clapped.

The multicolored stage lights flash and the roar of the sold-out stadium crowd washes over international pop sensation EJ Payne. She looks out across the thousands of adoring eyes that are all waiting for her to perform. She flashes a bright smile and waves, sending the crowd into another wave of excitement.

"Any babysitters out there tonight?" EJ grips the microphone and points into the stands while the babysitters scream and whistle. "I'm dedicating this one to you babysitters—and the babies who need to burn up some energy before nap time!"

The spotlights swivel and the boppy music starts up. A special-effects machine blows white fog onto the stage, and it billows around EJ's ankles as she starts to sing, "Well, shake it up, baby, now! Twist and shout!"

EJ takes a breath before singing the next line, but coughs as she inhales some kind of powder from the fog. . . .

"Oh, no"—*cough, cough, sputter*—"Faith!" EJ let go of the vacuum handle that she'd been singing into like a microphone. Frustrated with herself for getting sucked into a daydream while babysitting, EJ took an open bottle of baby powder from Faith, who had been squeezing and shaking the powder so that thick clouds of white hung in the air. A fine layer of powder was quickly landing on every surface in the room.

"What a mess." EJ surveyed the destruction. Bert had had enough and shook the powder from his coat before trotting out of the room to go see what Isaac was up to.

"Meh." The powder in Faith's dark hair made her look like she was going gray. "Meh. Ssss."

"Faith, is that your first word?" EJ sat down next to her and brushed some of the powder out of Faith's hair. "Mess. Mess?"

"Meh. Sss." That was close enough to "mess" for EJ. She picked her sister up and gave her a big hug.

"You are the smartest baby ever in the history of babies!" EJ kissed the top of Faith's head, but as EJ pulled her face away, the gum in her mouth got stuck in the baby's spiky hair. Before EJ could even realize what had happened, Faith's chubby hand was squishing and mashing the gum into her hair. EJ couldn't even believe her eyes. How much more could go wrong during her first time babysitting?

Faith pulled her hand away from her head, causing a long strand of gooey, sticky gum to form from the wad in her hair. EJ grabbed another wet wipe and used it to wipe the gum from Faith's hand, but getting the matted gum out of her hair was going to be another thing altogether. She *had* to get everything under control—the animal cracker crumbs, the powder mess, and now the gum—before Mom or Dad got home. Otherwise she might become a famous babysitter—but only famous for having the shortest babysitting career ever.

"Infant Home Care Assistant Isaac," EJ called. "I need you, please!"

EJ flipped though *Babysitting 101*, anxiously looking for something—anything—that could help get her out of this predicament. Aside from a short entry about permitting children to chew gum only with a parent's permission, there was nothing else about gum or gum removal that she could find.

"Give me some scissors." EJ spun around to see Isaac standing over Faith, surveying the glob of goo. "She'd look great with a bald spot. Might even start a trend."

"No! We're not cutting her hair!" EJ had flashbacks to Mom finding out that she'd accidentally cut a bald spot on Isaac's head when she was imagining that she was a world-famous hair stylist. "There's got to be another way." EJ scrunched her face and thought hard.

"Mrs. Winkle will know what to do!" EJ snatched the cordless phone from the table next to the rocking chair and pressed the speed-dial button for her neighbor's cell phone. The line made a clicking noise and went straight to voice mail. EJ ended the call and immediately dialed the Russells' home number. Macy always had good ideas and had even been in Girl Scouts for a couple of years. Maybe she could tell EJ how to remove gum from Faith's hair.

"You've reached the Russell residence." The recorded voices of all four Russells came through the phone's earpiece. "We're probably at one of Bryan's mathlete tournaments or at Macy's gymnastics competitions, but leave your name and number—" EJ pressed the red button to end the call.

Should she call Mom? No, this wasn't *really* an emergency. Faith wasn't hurt and she wasn't in any kind of danger—EJ watched as Faith clapped her hands and gleefully watched the excess baby powder fly into the air. And she *could* still salvage this babysitting fiasco, but not without help. She needed someone with excellent babysitting skills—someone who had done it all before. Someone. . . .

"CoraLee." EJ breathed the name and immediately knew that was who she should call. But what if CoraLee did nothing but make fun of her? Or what if she tattled on EJ to Mom? Would CoraLee even help her? EJ took a deep breath and punched the speed-dial button for the McCallisters. "Here goes nothin'."

Female Voice: Hello?
EJ: [nervously] Um, hi. Is this CoraLee?
Voice: No, this is her little sister, Katy. Who is this?
EJ: [relaxes] Oh, hi Katy. This is EJ.

Katy: EJ! Hi! How's it going? And why are you calling my sister?

Great, even Katy thinks this is totally weird, EJ thought.

EJ: Well, see, I need. . .her help with something. Would you put her on the phone?
Katy: CORALEE, EJ PAYNE IS ON THE PHONE FOR YOU!

EJ pulled the receiver away too late to avoid getting an earful of Katy's shout.

Katy: Here she is. [whispers] Don't let her give you a hard time.
CoraLee: Hello? EJ?
EJ: Hey, CoraLee. I'm babysitting for the first time tonight and long story short: Do you know how to get gum out of a baby's hair?
CoraLee: Maybe. Why should I help you?
EJ: Please, CoraLee. You've been babysitting for a long time now, and I'd really like to be as good as you, except I'll never get good unless I keep babysitting, and when Mom and Dad come home and see what a colossal mess I've made and the gum in Faith's hair, well, I just know that they'll never let me babysit again and actually right now I'm not sure I'm responsible enough to actually be a babysitter yet, but I don't want this one time to keep me from ever doing it again! And I . . .I could really use your help right now.

134

Katy: [on the other line] CoraLee, stop being such a meanie-face and go over there and help poor EJ!

CoraLee: Katy, I—

Katy: EJ, she knows exactly how to get gum out of hair because she let me chew some gum when she was babysitting and then it fell out of my mouth and got stuck in my hair while we were watching a DVD and she had to get it out before Mom came home. So, CoraLee, just for once in your life be a friend and help someone out! [Katy slams the phone down in a huff.]

EJ: Um.

CoraLee: Get some mayonnaise out of the refrigerator. I'll ride my bike and cut through a couple of backyards. I can be there in six minutes.

The line went dead.

EJ looked up from the phone and smiled. "Faith, I think CoraLee is about to save my babysitting behind."

Six minutes later, CoraLee swooped into the Payne house and with the expertise of a seasoned babysitter, showed EJ how to massage a glob of mayo into Faith's hair. And in just a few minutes, EJ was able to remove the matted gum with the help of the creamy, white sandwich spread—it was kind of like magic, really.

Faith splashed and squealed in the bath as she played with a family of multicolored rubber ducks while EJ and CoraLee sat on the edge of the tub. Two doors down, Isaac was in the nursery, on animal cracker and baby powder vacuuming duty. (EJ had to promise him his own pack of Double Stuf Oreos after this night was over.)

"CoraLee, thanks for your help." EJ said. "I wasn't sure you'd actually come over."

"Well, I probably wouldn't have—except I remembered what you said to me in our babysitting class after that ridiculous robo baby's head came off," CoraLee said. "You said nice things to me when you saw I was embarrassed in front of those older girls. You were nice even after I had been nasty to you. And, well. . ."

"Hey, what's going on in here—bathtime?" Mom popped her head through the bathroom doorway. "Oh, hi, CoraLee." Mom gave EJ a look that EJ clearly read as *CoraLee is visiting? This is new. . . .*"

"Hi, Mrs. Payne." CoraLee wiped her hands on a towel. "EJ asked me to come over because she just needed a little babysitter backup. And we infant home care professionals need to stick together, right, EJ?"

EJ nodded, speechless.

"EJ is an excellent babysitter, Mrs. Payne. Very patient and levelheaded. Faith is lucky to have her."

"And me—the infant home care assistant!" Isaac ran past the open bathroom door, shoving an Oreo in his mouth.

"Sounds like you all had an eventful evening," Mom said. "Did you have fun with your big sis, Faith?"

"Meh. Sss!" Faith pounded the tub water with a rubber duck in each hand, sending a cascade of water on EJ's lap.

EJ shook her head and grinned. "Yes, Faith. Mess is right."

Chapter 11

The ~~Bachelorette~~ Spinster Party

Dear Diary,

Tonight is a first for me—I'm going to Mrs. Winkle's bachelorette party!

Well, *technically* it's not a bachelorette party. According to the invitation, it's a *spinster* party. Mrs. Winkle hand-delivered the invitations to us a couple of weeks ago, popping in the back door during breakfast.

Mrs. Winkle: [hands invitations to Mom and me] Here you are, dears! Invitations to my spinster party!

Mom: Wilma! [laughs] You are *not* a spinster!

Mrs. Winkle: [smiles] I most certainly *am* a spinster, Tabby. I fit the very definition: an older woman who has never married and has no children. But my Prince Charming, Mr. Johnson, will soon rescue me from spinsterhood.

(Side note: Even though Mr. Johnson is way better now than he ever was as the neighborhood grump, I would *never* describe him as "Prince Charming." But I have to admit that it is pretty sweet how Mrs. Winkle's face lights up so beautifully when she talks about him. Love is a mystery, Diary.)

Mrs. Winkle: Anyway, my lovelies, doesn't a spinster party sound better than the other option—an old maid party?

Me: It does sound better, but Old Maid *is* one of my favorite card games!

Mrs. Winkle: Great minds think alike, EJ. Playing Old Maid is absolutely on the agenda for my spinster party.

Mom: Well, girls, this sounds like a bachelorette party that we won't soon forget.

Mrs. Winkle: *Spinster* party, dear. Embrace the word! Spinster!

A few years ago when I found out that Mrs. Winkle had never been married, I asked her why she was called Mrs. instead of Miss or Ms. Her answer was so delightfully Winklely: "My first year of teaching art at Spooner Elementary, there was a typo on the nameplate on my classroom door," she said. "And once I heard my students call me 'Mrs.' I realized I liked the sound of four syllables in my teacher name instead of three—Missus Winkle is just so much more melodic than Miss Winkle. So I decided to stick with Mrs., and that's what I've been called ever since."

Apparently Mrs. Winkle has always been a woman who knows what she wants, and it's one of the reasons I love her (and want to be just like her when I grow up).

So Mom, Faith, Macy (Mrs. Winkle said I could invite a friend!), and I will party hard with Mrs. Winkle tonight. In two short weeks, her name will legally change to Mrs. Johnson. But truthfully, Diary, she'll always be Mrs. Winkle in my heart.

EJ

"Aw, nuts!" Macy looked up from the playing card she'd just drawn from EJ's hand. "Old Maid!"

EJ smiled as she laid down her final pair of cards—two matching mail carriers—on the coffee table in Mrs. Winkle's living room, clinching the win. "Good game, Mace," she said, collecting the cards into a stack and away from Faith, who was making a toddley beeline toward them as she rounded the coffee table. EJ knew Faith would love nothing more than to rip the deck of cards into 857 tiny pieces.

"Ladies, please make yourselves at home." Mrs. Winkle glided into the living room and set a final tray of snacks on the small buffet table against the wall. The party guests gathered around to chat and enjoy the finger foods and dainty desserts. Along with EJ, Macy, Mom, and Faith, other party guests included Miss Adele and two other ladies from Mrs. Winkle's bowling league.

"How are the wedding preparations coming, Wilma?" Miss Adele asked, between bites of a cranberry-orange scone. "Is the theme still a top secret?"

"Everything's going according to plan." Mrs. Winkle adjusted her tiara that spelled out the word *spinster* in multicolored gems. "And yes, it's a secret. I decided it would be fun to surprise everyone on the big day. But all of you will get to help with a very important part of the plans tonight—"

"The *men* are crashing this *women* party!" Isaac's voice burst through the front door before his body did. All eyes in the room swiveled toward Mrs. Winkle's front door as it swung open and Isaac bounded in, flexing his arms. "Here comes the macho muscle!" The ladies in the room tittered in amused chuckles.

"Oh, it's my favorite little man!" Mrs. Winkle smooshed

Isaac's cheeks between her hands, and Isaac grinned, making him look like a chipmunk. Mrs. Winkle had a way of doing things that would be hugely annoying if any other adult did them, but somehow they weren't annoying and she made you feel special when she did them. Isaac threw his arms around Mrs. Winkle's waist and hugged her tight as Mr. Johnson and Dad trailed behind Isaac, making a much less impressive entrance into the house.

"We're going to the arcade for Mr. Johnson's bachelor party!" Isaac announced. "And I get to spend ten *whole* dollars' worth of quarters!" Isaac jingled the forty quarters in his pants pockets to prove it. Secretly, EJ was a little jealous. She loved the arcade—especially skee-ball.

"I'm gonna teach these young gunslingers how it's done in the arcade's old-time shooting gallery," Mr. Johnson said, aiming his cane like a shotgun at a nearby lamp. "I wonder if my top score from 1963 is still on the leader's board."

"Whoa." EJ did a quick calculation and whispered to Macy, "That's more than forty years ago. Mr. Johnson is o-l-d."

"If your name isn't there anymore, you'll just have to set a new record tonight, dear." Mrs. Winkle pecked a kiss on Mr. Johnson's cheek. "Go easy on these two. They're inexperienced."

"Hey! I—" Dad stopped short and picked up Faith, who was running toward him with her arms outstretched. "Oh, who am I kidding? You're right, Wilma, I can't hit the broad side of a barn."

"All right, you macho muscle, time for you to go to your own party." Mom took Faith from Dad, and the toddler took the cue to start waving bye to the men. "Have a fun evening."

Isaac made pistols with his fingers and jingled his quarters as the three men (*two men and one wanna-be*, EJ thought) said their good-byes and left.

"Girls, it's time for the big event of the evening!" Mrs. Winkle rubbed her palms together in eager anticipation.

"Games?" one of the bowling ladies asked.

"A game of sorts, but more of a contest." Mrs. Winkle's eyes twinkled, and she winked at EJ. "If everyone will follow me to the basement, we can get started."

Mrs. Winkle's basement—her art studio—was absolutely the best spot in the house. Wilma Winkle thrived on creating new and exciting (and usable and wearable and sometimes even edible) art. "I am always amazed by the beauty of God's creation," she'd told EJ once. "When I am making a piece of art, I talk to God and thank Him for all the weird and wonderful things He made for us to enjoy." But Mrs. Winkle not only loved *making* art, she loved encouraging creativity in others, too, which was why she'd made such a great teacher.

EJ had spent some of the best hours of her life with Mrs. Winkle in her basement studio. From magazine collages and watercolor to clay sculpting and stained glass art, they had done it all. But EJ's absolute favorite memory in the art studio was the time when Mrs. Winkle invited the Paynes over one evening and told them to wear clothes that they didn't mind ruining. When they arrived, they found Mrs. Winkle had covered every square inch of the art studio in white paper, and she had more than a dozen spray bottles, each filled with a different paint color. The only instruction Mrs. Winkle gave was, "Go!" and what transpired was a glorious mess of color, laughter, and a story that they would talk about for years to come. Now each of them had a small framed sample of the giant canvas to remember the fun they had. EJ's hung on the wall next to her bed.

"Here we are!" Mrs. Winkle flipped on the studio's light switch to show. . .well, EJ wasn't quite sure what to make of what she saw in front of her. Four Hula-Hoops leaned against a giant plastic shopping bag full of feathers of all colors. A stack of newspapers and magazines. A shoe box full of buttons and Ping-Pong balls. A crate full of different kinds of ribbons. Empty paper towel and toilet paper rolls. Several bolts of fabric in bright colors. A cardboard box filled with packing peanuts and bubble wrap. And a sewing box overflowing with scissors, tape measures, pins, thread, and duct tape—rolls and rolls of duct tape in lots of patterns and colors.

"Um, what are we looking at?" Macy bit a fingernail nervously. She was a Mrs. Winkle art rookie. "What do you think the contest is going to be?"

EJ was immediately drawn to the bag of feathers of all shapes and sizes. "I have no idea, but the possibilities are *endless!*"

"Here's the contest, ladies—make an outfit from anything you can find in the room. You have fifteen minutes." Macy and a couple of the bowling ladies looked uneasy, but EJ was ready to go—this was Winkle fun at its finest. "Ready, set, create!"

EJ's pencil hovers over her fashion sketchbook and waits for inspiration to strike. She is the very best, most talented fashion designer in all of Los Angeles, and her stylish studio in sunny Beverly Hills is buzzing with activity as actresses hunt for the perfect dress for the upcoming awards season.

Designing for the Hollywood star, Miss Macy Russell, however, is proving to be a challenge for her. EJ crumples her current sketch and tosses it over her left shoulder, landing in a pile of fabric scraps. A clean slate, that's what she needs.

"Miss Russell, would you mind throwing a handful of feathers into

the air?" EJ points to a bag of feathers next to Macy.

"Throw them?" Macy sounded shocked that EJ would suggest such a thing. "I don't want to make a mess in Mrs. Winkle's house."

"No, no, dear!" Mrs. Winkle called from across the room where she was helping a couple of the bowling ladies make a skirt out of Hula-Hoops, bubble wrap, and orange duct tape. "Messes are what the studio is for. The very best art comes from the messiest mess!"

"Yes ma'am." Macy grinned at EJ as she clawed two handfuls of feathers from the bag.

An explosion of fluff and color shoots straight into the air and hangs for a split second before the shower of feathers falls to the floor— some twirling, others floating softly on a passing air current, a few landing quickly, as though gravity has a stronger hold on them than it has on the others. All activity in the studio seems to stop as every eye watches the simple but beautiful mess take shape.

"Perfect!" Inspiration strikes, and EJ's colored pencils dance on her sketchbook. The studio resumes its buzz as glamorous garments take shape. A minute later, EJ finishes her sketch with a flurry and turns the paper to show her famous client. "Voilà! What do you think? I know you will love it! It is the best I have ever done, if I do say so myself."

Macy excitedly takes the sketch from EJ, but her face quickly changes from eager to confused. "It certainly is a good picture. . . ." Macy turns the sketch toward EJ. "But this is a sketch of a peacock. I thought you were sketching my dress."

"Macy, my dear Macy, you must trust me!" EJ grips Macy's shoulders and looks her straight in the eye. "I have a vision, and this peacock is the inspiration for the most perfect dress ever made!" Before Macy can reply, EJ snatches the sketch and pins it to the wall.

"I trust you, madam designer." Macy gives the peacock sketch one more sideways glance before nodding at EJ. "Do your stuff."

EJ drapes a measuring tape around her shoulders, and adds a white feather boa to get her in the feather mood. Proving once and for all that she's not a diva in the slightest, Macy offers to help, and EJ gives her the job of sorting the bag of feathers by color. EJ quickly cuts pieces of green fabric and pins together a simple knee-length dress on Macy.

"Now's when the real magic begins." EJ loosely ties a scrap of fabric around Macy's head like a blindfold so she can't see the dress till the big reveal.

EJ begins her work in a flurry of feathers. She starts at the top of the dress with striking dark blue feathers, and as she moves down, she uses lighter blues that lead into greens, and then pink, next purple, and finally to a deep red at along the hem of the skirt. She whistles as she works, answering Macy's questions of "How does it look?" "Exactly as I pictured it!" and "How much longer?" "Just a few more minutes."

As a final touch, EJ creates a stunning feathered headpiece that she pins to Macy's hair before stepping back and admiring the finished product.

"Lovely, simply lovely. The best I've ever done." EJ leads the still-blindfolded Macy to stand in front of a full-length mirror. "Fun, fabulous feathers, with just the right amount of bird." EJ removes the cloth from Macy's eyes.

Macy peered at herself in the mirror, and a look of horror crossed her face as she took in the mishmash of feather boas and loose craft feathers haphazardly pinned to her clothes, sticking out at awkward angles. Macy's reaction to the outfit was exactly what EJ was hoping for—the outfit she'd just created in twelve minutes looked like something only a crazy person would wear.

"It's. . .interesting." Macy didn't want to hurt her best friend's feelings.

"I call it the 'insane peacock'!" EJ laughed, breaking the tension Macy was feeling.

"Oh, EJ, I look hilarious!" Macy laughed and turned a circle to take in all the crazy that was happening on her outfit. "I could pass as Big Bird's weird cousin."

Faith made a squawking noise that sounded very birdlike from the Pack 'N Play a few feet away, which made EJ and May laugh even harder.

"Time's up!" Mrs. Winkle called. "Judging will begin now."

Mrs. Winkle walked around the room to take a close look at what everyone had made. Mom modeled a garbage bag shirt that was belted with a blue duct tape belt and a striped skirt made out of several different colors of duct tape. Miss Adele's bubble wrap and Hula-Hoop skirt had become a full-fledged ball gown, although EJ thought it looked pretty uncomfortable.

"Lovely! Simply superb!" Mrs. Winkle gushed. When she caught a glimpse of EJ's creation, Mrs. Winkle gasped. "Oh, girls, this feathered ensemble is positively inspired. *This* is what my wedding dress will be."

EJ was sure she must've heard Mrs. Winkle wrong.

"You're going to wear *that*?" EJ pointed at the outfit that looked like a pile of molting bird feathers. "But. . .you can't! It's your wedding. You have to wear a *wedding* dress!"

If only Mrs. Winkle had explained the contest more thoroughly, EJ would've designed something completely different!

"Oh, now, EJ, I think we've always known that I wouldn't be a traditional bride." Mrs. Winkle smiled.

A clump of feathers fell off of Macy's dress, leaving a large bald spot on her left hip.

What had EJ done?

Chapter 12

Espionage Ear Piercing

Dear Diary,

After six long years of asking (and begging) to get my ears
pierced, I'm finally allowed to get it done—and
today is the day—just in time for the wedding
next weekend!

  Mom and Dad have always said that having
pierced ears is a big responsibility and that I
would be allowed to get it done when I was old enough.
(Dad actually said once that I wouldn't be allowed to pierce
my ears until I turned thirty, Diary! Thirty! That's positively
ANCIENT!) Macy got her ears pierced when she was five,
and she never had any problems. So for a long time I thought
it was supremely unfair that Mom and Dad were so firm
about not letting me do it, too. But one time when I was in
an extra-whiney mood about it, Mom told me the story of
she got her ears pierced when she was only six years old, and
they got so painfully infected that she had to go to the doctor
to get antibiotics AND she had to let the holes grow shut so
the infection could heal completely. ("She was lucky the doctor
didn't have to amputate her ears," Dad teased. At least I *hope*
he was teasing.) Mom said the experience was so bad that

for more than ten years, she didn't even *want* to get her ears pierced. Finally when she was in college she got them pierced again, but she was extra careful about keeping her piercings and earrings clean so that she didn't get another infection.

Mom and I are going to The Golden Jewelry Company in downtown Spooner to get it done. It's the same place where Dad and Mom bought their wedding rings for each other and where they bought the silver star-shaped locket necklace that they surprised me with two Christmases ago. The owners of the shop, Mr. and Mrs. Golden, go to our church, and they are pretty cool. They're originally from Germany, but they've lived in the United States for longer than I've been alive. I love listening to their German accents, and sometimes it makes me wish that I spoke with an accent.

So the next time I write in you, I will be more holy. Okay, okay—that's a corny preacher's kid joke. Maybe that should be spelled "hole-y." Time to fulfill a lifelong dream!

EJ

EJ tried to imagine a much younger Mom and Dad standing at the display case in the small jewelry shop, pointing and wishing and dreaming of the rings they were choosing for each other for their wedding. It was strange to think of them before they were married. They weren't Mom and Dad (yet)—they were just David and Tabitha, brand-new adults and recent college graduates. EJ couldn't wait until she was twenty-three and all the cool things she'd be able to do then.

But first things first. Time to get her ears pierced.

"What about these sparkly ones?" Mom tapped the glass case, pointing to a pair of imitation diamond stud earrings.

"Maybe." EJ's eyes scanned the row of options until her eyes landed on the perfect pair—tiny silver stars. "Stars! Winner winner, chicken dinner."

"Good choice." Mom grinned. "On the earrings and giving me a suggestion for what we should get for supper tonight. We haven't had fried chicken in a long time."

"Are vee all set?" Mrs. Golden appeared on the other side of the display. EJ nodded and pointed at her selection. "Oh, zees are lovely. You haf excellent taste, EJ. Come, I vill set up a piercing station in zee back."

"Do you need me to come, EJ?" Mom asked EJ quietly as Mrs. Golden made her way to the back of the shop. "I will come back if you want me to."

"No, Mom, it's fine. I can do it by myself." EJ believed the words, even though her stomach did a little flip as she said them. She rounded the display case and followed Mrs. Golden through a doorway, turning back to flash Mom a thumbs-up before ducking inside.

"Haf a seat." Mrs. Golden motioned to a molded plastic chair and turned toward a cabinet from which she produced a silver tool that looked like a cross between a paper hole puncher and a plastic gun. Was that what she would use to pierce EJ's ears? EJ started breathing a little faster.

"So, EJ, vat grade are you in now?" Mrs. Golden's small talk was friendly as she set the tool on the table.

"Fifth." EJ could only squeak out a one-word answer in between her rapid breathing.

"And how is zee baby?" Mrs. Golden opened another drawer, looking for something. "Vat is her name again? Joy? Hope?"

EJ had to swallow the lump in her throat just to get the single word out this time. "F–Faith." What was wrong with her? EJ rarely had a problem talking to. . .anyone. Mom always said she had the gift of gab. EJ felt silly that she was so nervous. As if on cue, her hands started shaking.

"Yes, Faith. Zat's right. Such a beautiful name." Mrs. Golden turned toward EJ, looked over the top of her reading glasses, and smiled. "I just need to sanitize zee studs and zen vee vill be ready to go. Be back in two shakes of a lamb's tail."

EJ's breathing slowed a bit as she watched Mrs. Golden leave the room until her eyes fell back on the gun-like object left on the table. EJ tucked her hands under her legs to get them to stop shaking and tried to think of anything else.

CIA Operative EJ Payne is in a pickle. Not that she hasn't been in pickles before, but this was a pickle of international importance.

After years of working undercover under assumed identities, the underground criminal network known simply as the Baddies have finally caught up with her. And now they've tied her up and locked her in a room and are letting her sweat a little. But she isn't worried. She won't talk. No matter what they do to her, she won't betray her country.

"Vell now, here vee are." An older woman enters the room. EJ scoffs as she realizes the mastermind Baddies in charge won't be giving her the pleasure of defeating them face-to-face.

"So they send a grandma to do the dirty work?" EJ asks.

"Oh yes, I do love my grandchildren," she says. "But zis is not dirty work. Everyzing is very clean."

EJ furrows her brow, trying to figure out what the woman's code words could mean as the Baddie picks up the gun to load it. Nervous sweat drips down EJ's back as she watches the woman put on a pair of plastic gloves and then cracks her knuckles menacingly.

"What do you want?" EJ asks between clenched teeth.

"Vee'll need payment, of course," the woman says. "But vee vill vork somezing out."

EJ strains against the rope that's holding her to the chair. A wave of hope rushes over her as she feels the knots loosen a bit.

"You vill need to sit still, Miss Payne." The woman shines a light directly into EJ's eyes, and she squints. The woman grips the gun in her right hand and leans over EJ. EJ holds her breath and her mind whirs, trying to plan her next move as she sees the sharp end of the weapon move closer and closer to her skin. "Zis is going to hurt."

"AHHHH!" EJ's reflexes overtook her self-control, and her hands flew from under her legs to cover her ears and she shut her eyes tight. "No! I won't reveal my secrets, Baddie! But please don't hurt me!"

Shocked, Mrs. Golden stepped back and set the piercing gun on the worktable behind her, out of EJ's sight. "Dear child, I'm not going to hurt you!" Mrs. Golden kneeled on the floor and put a comforting hand on EJ's shoulder. "EJ, are you all right?"

EJ opened her eyes and met Mrs. Golden's kind gaze and smiled weakly.

"Everything okay in there?" Mom's voice floated through the door. "I thought I heard yelling."

EJ felt a blush creep into her cheeks. What a baby she was.

"Don't vorry," Mrs. Golden called. "EJ was just acting out a scene from a movie for me. Vee are almost done here. Be out in a minute."

The sound of Mom's footsteps faded as she walked away from the door.

Mrs. Golden rose from the floor, opened a cabinet door, and started pulling things out.

"You know, EJ, it's okay to admit ven you're scared," Mrs. Golden said. "You might just find zat someone can help you. Do you still vant to get your ears pierced?"

"Yes, I do, Mrs. Golden." EJ had finally found her voice. "I'll try not to freak out this time."

"I haf a friend who vill help you. He's helped dozens of girls get their ears pierced," she said, reaching to the very back of the cabinet. "And not just kids, either—grown ladies. A few months ago, he helped a voman who got her ears pierced for her fiftieth birthday! Ah, zere you are, Mr. Snuggles!"

Mrs. Golden pulled a giant teddy bear—twice the size of Faith—out of the cabinet and waved him at EJ. "Just close your eyes, squeeze zis guy tight, and it'll be over before you know it."

EJ took Mr. Snuggles from Mrs. Golden and immediately felt better with his soft fur against her arms and face. She could do it.

"Okay, I'm ready. Except—" EJ hesitated for a moment. "Could we just keep the Mr. Snuggles part of the ear piercing a secret? I have a certain reputation to uphold."

"Your secret is safe vith me, EJ." Mrs. Golden smiled.

Chapter 13

THE CLOSET MONSTER

Dear Diary,

My homework is done, pajamas are on, teeth are brushed, good-nights are hugged, prayers are said, and I'm in my bed at 8:07 p.m.—a full fifty-three minutes before my actual bedtime.

Why am I going to bed so early? Because tomorrow is Mrs. Winkle's wedding! I can't wait to do my part as her junior bridesmaid, and I'm dying to see what amazingly creative things she has planned for the wedding. So I want it to be tomorrow already— as in, right now. And the fastest way to bring tomorrow is to go to sleep!

On a normal night, I try to work the system to stay up as late as possible. I mean, honestly, Diary, I think every kid does this. When I was in kindergarten, I was convinced that Mom and Dad were having crazy fun parties without me after I went to bed. And when I whined about it enough, Mom

finally gave in and let me stay up one night. Let me tell you, Diary. . . . It was hands-down the most boringest "party" ever: Dad worked on an adult Sunday school lesson in his home office, and Mom clipped coupons at the kitchen table. I gave up after twenty minutes and put myself to bed.

But even though Mom and Dad are a big yawn-fest after lights-out, I still usually want to stay up—hey, all I need is a good book to have an EJ party! And after years of practice I know all the tricks:

* I need a drink of water or I will die of dehydration.

* Whoops! I forgot to brush my teeth. . .

* . . .(followed immediately by) I still need to floss. Dentist's orders.

* Please may I read *one* more chapter? I have to know what happens!

* Bert needs to go outside one more time or else I'll have a mess to clean up.

* I'm five years older than Isaac. I should be allowed at least twenty more minutes of TV! (That one never works.)

So the fact that I've gone to bed tonight without putting up any fight must've been a welcome change of pace for Mom and Dad. When I gave Mom a good-night kiss at 7:54 p.m., she asked me if I was feeling all right and laid her hand on my forehead to check for a fever. I told her yes, I'm fine. Just excited. And when I hugged Dad good-night, he actually asked me to pinch him because he said he thought for sure he must be dreaming. I laughed and pinched his arm (but not too hard) and confirmed that he was awake.

EJ

EJ punched her pillow, which was feeling lumpier than normal, and flopped her head back down. Her eyes, no matter how hard she tried, simply would not stay shut. And the big, red 8:35 p.m. on the alarm clock sitting atop her bedside table seemed strangely brighter than usual.

Lying near her feet, Bert let out a sigh to let EJ know he was still awake, too. . .and apparently bored.

"It feels like going to bed early is actually making tomorrow come slower." EJ turned on a small reading lamp clipped to the headboard of her bed. "What should we do?"

Bert's head popped up and eagerly looked around the room for something fun. He jumped off the bed and picked up EJ's ukulele case by the strap and brought it back, looking up at her.

"You want me to play, Bert?" EJ took the instrument from him and the dog joined her on the bed, snuggling in next to her. "I suppose I *could* use some more practice before my big performance in the wedding tomorrow."

EJ began strumming the opening chords to "You Are My Sunshine" and Bert happily laid his chin on her knee, enjoying the serenade. EJ sang to him, "You are my sunshine, my only sunshine. You make me happy when skies are gray. You'll never know, dear, how much I love you. Please don't take my sunshine away."

EJ was glad that this was the song that Mrs. Winkle wanted her to play as she walked down the aisle. It wasn't mushy and love-y and gross. It was simple and nice—the kind of song she could sing to her dog or to a friend. And that's what Mrs. Winkle and Mr. Johnson had become—friends. It seemed like such a long time ago that Mr. Johnson had been nothing but the neighborhood grump, shouting at EJ and sending his attack cat, Gruff, after her when she would try to cut through his yard as a shortcut to the park.

But Mrs. Winkle had seen past Mr. Johnson's mean outside and found a person who was really rather splendid on the inside. Kind of like how EJ had seen glimpses of a nice person inside CoraLee (when she chose to let the nice person out). And even Isaac wasn't so bad when he was drugged up and telling EJ how much he really liked her and the only reason he spent so much time annoying her was to get her attention.

EJ strummed her uke absentmindedly and hummed as Bert dozed beside her, jealous that he was already asleep and wondering if she was tired enough to drift off yet. She leaned back against her pillow and gazed at her junior bridesmaid dress, hanging on a hook on the back of her closet door. Dresses weren't EJ's favorite thing to wear—she'd much rather have on a comfy pair of old jeans, a T-shirt, and her All-Star Converse sneakers—but she had to admit that she looked nice in the pale yellow knee-length dress and ballet flats.

EJ looked at her alarm clock—8:55 p.m. She decided to read a couple chapters from *The Horse and His Boy* by C. S. Lewis by flashlight under the covers before calling it a night.

As often happened when EJ read a great book, she got completely sucked into the story of the adventures in Narnia and was surprised to realize that she had read six whole chapters. She peeked her head out of the covers to see that her alarm clock read 2:26 a.m. Bert was well into his trip to Dreamsville and was currently licking his paw like it was the most delicious dog bone he'd ever tasted. EJ sincerely hoped he wouldn't start gnawing on his own leg.

Just as EJ was about to turn off her flashlight and try to join Bert in Dreamsville, she heard a shuffling sound on the other side of the small door that joined her room to Isaac's room. She got up quietly to investigate.

When EJ and Isaac were little, the door was a "secret passage" that they would use to crawl through the door between their rooms while they played. It was fun until the day Isaac sneaked through to scare EJ and her friends during a slumber party. Since then, EJ had kept the door locked on her side.

EJ pressed her ear to the door and the muffled sound of Isaac's voice floated through. She could still hear the fear in her brother's whispery voice.

"It's not real. Just go to sleep. It's not real."

She normally couldn't hear her brother in his room unless he was jumping on the bed or being extra loud and crazy. She assumed he must be near the door for her to hear him so clearly.

"You're a big, tough guy, Isaac, so don't be scared," he said in a deep voice that EJ recognized as the one Isaac used when he played with his favorite T-Rex figurine.

"But what if that thing comes out and gets me while I'm sleeping?" Isaac responded in his own voice, sniffling. "I need some help. . .but who will help me?"

EJ thought that Isaac talking to himself probably wasn't a good sign. And was he crying? The kid had a lot of faults, but he generally didn't cry much or get scared of silly things. She glanced back at her bed, wondering if she should let this play out by itself or try to help her brother. It seemed like it might have the potential to be an adventure like Isaac loved to have with his sister. . . .

EJ quietly turned the doorknob, unlocking it, and pulled it open. Isaac, along with a blanket and pillow, tumbled backward into EJ's room with a surprised yelp.

"Shh! Isaac, what are you doing?" EJ whispered, hoping Mom and Dad didn't hear the commotion. She shined the beam of her flashlight on her brother's face. "Why are you sleeping on the floor against the door?"

"I'm trying to get away from him." Isaac's eyes were wide with fear, and he definitely looked like he'd been crying.

"Him? Him who?" EJ's heart lurched. "Is there someone in your room?"

Isaac pointed toward his open closet door. "There's someone in there, and he's talking to me."

EJ shined her flashlight toward the dark closet and took two steps into Isaac's room. Isaac stood beside her and peered toward the closet, but all the small beam showed was a space that was very full of toys and clothes—desperately needing to be cleaned out. Isaac had a bad habit of "cleaning" his room by shoving everything into the closet and simply shutting the door. The last time he'd done that, he couldn't get the closet door to shut completely, and it now stood partially open.

"Isaac, I don't think anyone could even fit in that closet," EJ whispered. "Are you sure it's not just your imagination? Trust me, I know a thing or two about imaginations running away with themselves."

As if on cue, an eerie crackle of static came from deep inside Isaac's closet followed by a deep, distorted voice: *"No escape. . . . Destroy you."*

Isaac scrambled behind EJ, tripping the door between their rooms so it snapped shut with a *click*. EJ grabbed the doorknob a second too late. Locked. EJ knocked on the door as loudly as she dared and called for Bert, but she could hear his soft snores on her

164

bed from the other side of the door. The dog could sleep through a marching band coming through the room, EJ was convinced. The only way out was to walk past the closet and whoever—whatever—was inside.

"De. . .stroy. De. . .stroy."

"It's going to destroy me!" Isaac squeaked, burying his face in EJ's back. "W–what do we do, EJ?"

EJ hesitated. Logically, she knew that whatever scary sounds were coming out of the closet, it wasn't *actually* a monster—but that didn't do much to make the situation less frightening. If they could get past the closet, they could at least turn on the lights and see what was really going on. . . .

"What I like the most is when we imagine together, EJ." Isaac's voice from his laughing gas-induced state at the dentist office popped in her head. This was a prime imagination opportunity that Isaac might talk about during his next cavity filling.

"Isaac, this is what you've been training for." EJ turns and grips the young cadet by the shoulders. "You can't let this opportunity pass you by, or you'll never graduate from the Monster Exterminator Academy. And you'll regret it for the rest of your life."

EJ has been Isaac's mentor during his time at MEA, and Isaac has always shown such promise in his practice drills. Big-eyed aliens, slimy, snakelike ghouls, giant, hairy beasts with razor-sharp fangs—Isaac had aced every scenario EJ threw at him. But that was in the simulator. This is real life.

"You're better at this stuff than I am, EJ," Isaac says. "I'll just follow you like I usually do, okay?"

"Come on, I believe you can do it, Isaac," EJ says. "And you won't be alone. I'll be right here with you."

"You will?" Isaac's eyes are unsure. *"I thought I would have to do it myself to graduate the academy."*

"This is what being on a team is all about." EJ thrusts the laser destroyer toward the cadet. *"We're here for each other. I've got your back, cadet."*

"Okay, I can do it." Isaac accepts the laser destroyer from EJ and gives a sharp salute before taking a confident step forward—EJ right behind him.

Isaac gives the hand signal to EJ to move forward. Perfectly in sync, they walk ahead on silent feet. Two menacing, red eyes peer out of the monster's lair, sensing the threat of the exterminators coming to end him.

Sssspptt-pop. *"Join us, or die."* Crack-crack-crack. *"You are beaten. It is useless to resist."*

"I won't join you." Isaac's voice sounds confident. *"I am not afraid, and I will destroy you."*

"Good!" EJ whispers to Isaac, urging him on. *"Now find his weakness and attack it."*

Crackity-snap. *"Only. . .hatred will destroy me."* Pop-pop.

Suddenly Isaac spins toward EJ, the light of an idea on his face.

"EJ, we have to show the monster that we like it! We have to do the opposite of what he says!" Isaac's eyes are bright. *"Sing him the song."*

"Are you sure, cadet?" Isaac isn't following normal exterminator procedure, and it's making EJ nervous.

"I'm sure. Sing!"

EJ begins to softly sing "You Are My Sunshine," and the monster goes silent. As the evil creature is distracted by the song, Isaac takes a flying leap into the cave and aims his laser destroyer at the red eyes. Isaac yelps as a booby trap the monster set lets loose with an avalanche of rocks. He jumps out of the way and snatches the monster by the head, unleashing the laser destroyer into the right eye of the creature as he tucks and rolls out of the cave.

"*The force is strong with this one.*" Sssspptt-pop. "*You have. . . controlled your. . .feeeear.*"

Finally on the far side of Isaac's room, EJ snapped on the light switch to find Isaac on the floor, shining the flashlight directly into the eye of his Darth Vader voice simulator helmet—the very same one that he'd used to scare EJ's friends at her ninth birthday slumber party—and looking entirely pleased with himself. The batteries were apparently dying in it, and it gave a pathetic little "Luke, I am your fatherrrrrrr" before sputtering static to silence.

"How was that thing talking without someone wearing it?" EJ never did like that mask much, so she was happy to hear it take its last breath.

"The switch was flipped to store display mode." Isaac looked up from the now-lifeless mask. "And look—it was sitting on top of one of my light-up sneakers. That's what made the eyes glow red."

EJ looked at the hunk of black plastic in Isaac's hands. They both felt a little silly for being so scared of a toy.

"That was pretty great, Isaac. I'm proud of you," EJ said, taking the mask, popping the batteries out (just to be safe), and tossing it into Isaac's closet before shoving the door closed with her hip. "How did that dream rate for you?"

"Maybe the best one ever," Isaac said as he hopped into bed, tucking his T-Rex in beside him. "I like it when we're on the same team instead of against each other, EJ."

"Yeah, we do make a pretty good team, kid." EJ cracked open Isaac's bedroom door and looked over her shoulder at him. "Good night."

Chapter 14

THE BIG DAY

Dear Diary,

Today's the day I've been waiting for since two Thanksgivings ago when Mr. Johnson and Mrs. Winkle started flirting with each other! (P.S. gross) Being in a wedding is one of those things that I've been dying to do ever since I first saw *The Sound of Music* wedding scene where Liesl, Louisa, Brigitta, Marta, and Gretl marched down the aisle in front of the beautiful bride, Maria. It is, in two words, simply lovely.

We Paynes all have pretty important roles to play in the wedding today. Me as the junior bridesmaid and "bridal procession musician" (I gave myself that second title), Dad as the pastor (a role he's used to playing), Faith and Bert will tag-team as the most adorable flower girl-slash-dog team in the world (if everything goes as planned with those two, it will be magical—if not, it could be a disaster), Isaac as the ring bearer and reception comedian (yes, it's still a thing), and Mom as the "kid wrangler." ("Somebody's got to keep everyone in line!" she said.)

Right now, though, my main problem is that I'm not sure I'm going to be able to keep my eyes open for the whole wedding, Diary. Why am I so tired? I didn't sleep much last night because I stayed up too late reading and then Isaac and I had to defeat Darth Vader in an epic battle of good versus evil. By the time I sneaked back to my room, got into bed, and finally settled down after the excitement, my clock said 2:48 a.m.

The last time I looked at the clock, it was 3:36 a.m., Diary. And I guess I must've fallen asleep after that, because the next thing I knew my alarm clock was squawking its terrible wake-up noise at 7:30 a.m.

I'm not allowed to drink coffee, and the one time Dad let me try a sip of his, I thought it was probably the most disgusting thing I'd ever tasted in my life. But today is one of those days that I think I could use some to help me stay awake.

My role in the wedding is so terribly important, Diary, and I want to do my very best for Mrs. Winkle. So I *have* to get it done. I was born for this, and I can do it. There's no way I am going to let her down.

It's almost time to go to the church. Here goes nothing.

EJ

EJ slouched in a rocking chair as Faith toddled around the Vine Street Community Church nursery in her pale pink flower girl dress, her hair in two tiny pigtails made with daisy hair ties. Even though Faith spent every Sunday in the church's nursery, the way she was squealing with excitement at each toy she laid eyes on made it seem like it was all new to her. Maybe the nursery was extra fun for her sister since there were no other little babies slobbering all over the toys, EJ thought. Any slobber that was on the toys today was all Faith.

EJ stifled a yawn, laid her head on the back of the chair, and soaked in the bright spring sunshine streaming through the nursery window. It really was a perfect day for a wedding. An especially ear-piercing squeal from the flower girl brought EJ's attention back to the tiny person in front of her, and she realized she was a little jealous of the toddler's energy from the full night of sleep she'd had. EJ honestly didn't know how she was going to stay awake today. Maybe she could slip away during the reception to get a little catnap under the back row of pews in the church's auditorium—her favorite hiding place in the building. Or maybe she could just close her eyes right now for a few minutes before. . . .

"Do you want to see Mrs. Winkle before the ceremony starts, EJ?" EJ's head snapped up, and she wiped a bead of drool that had formed in the corner of her mouth. She looked up to see Mom's eyes bright with excitement as she walked into the nursery, leading Bert on a leash.

EJ felt a surge of energy at the thought of seeing Mrs. Winkle. "Yes, please!" Mom took EJ's spot in the rocking chair to stay with Faith and Bert. EJ felt a few butterflies flit in her belly as she walked to the women's restroom just down the hall. If EJ's feather monstrosity from the spinster party was *actually* Mrs. Winkle's inspiration for her dress, EJ was afraid the bride was going to look completely ridiculous—and it would be all EJ's fault.

"Yes, I think one more pin should do the trick. Thank you, Adele." EJ followed Mrs. Winkle's voice past the row of sinks and found her standing in front of the bathroom's full-length mirror as Miss Adele attached a final bobby pin to secure the bride's veil. Mrs. Winkle saw EJ in the mirror and turned around with the biggest smile EJ had ever seen on her neighbor's face—so big that she didn't really even notice what her dress looked like at first. EJ hugged Mrs. Winkle tight.

"You look lovely, dear!" Mrs. Winkle kissed EJ on the forehead. "Just as I imagined you'd look—like the morning sunrise or a lovely little buttercup."

EJ grinned and stepped back to get a good look at Mrs. Winkle's dress. What she found made her extremely happy: Mrs. Winkle wore a simple knee-length dress made from a beautiful blue fabric—the same color as the bluebirds that roosted in the boxes in Mr. Johnson's backyard every spring. Just below the waist, the blue faded to a crisp white, and sewed along the hemline were tiny white feathers that swayed a bit when Mrs. Winkle moved. Pinned in her hair was a small white veil that covered just part of her face. But the best part of Mrs. Winkle's outfit was the short caplet made of soft blue feathers that she wore draped over her shoulders and tied around her neck with a white satin ribbon.

"Do you see how your dress from the spinster party inspired my look, EJ?" Mrs. Winkle smoothed a stray feather. "Until the party, I hadn't decided exactly how to decorate for the wedding, but your feather dress gave me the idea to pull everything together—in my wedding garden!"

"Your dress is *perfect*, Mrs. Winkle." EJ meant what she said, relieved her crazy creativity hadn't ruined the day. "But what do you mean your 'wedding garden'?"

Before Mrs. Winkle could explain, a loud knock sounded on the women's restroom door.

"Wilma?" Mr. Johnson called through the door. "Are you *sure* this is what I'm supposed to wear? It seems—I dunno— sacrilegious or something."

"Lester Johnson, don't you dare come in here!" Miss Adele leaned against the door in case he was going to try to come in. "You will *not* see the bride before the ceremony—it's bad luck!"

"Yeah, and this is the *girls'* bathroom, Mr. Johnson!" EJ added, giggling.

"EJ, please go out there and assure Lester that the outfit is the one I picked especially for him," Mrs. Winkle said. "And when you see what he's wearing, it might help you understand what I mean about my wedding garden."

EJ stepped into the hallway, expecting to see Mr. Johnson in a suit with multicolored flowers painted on it, or maybe a tux with a flowered shirt instead of the traditional white shirt, but what she saw instead was Mr. Johnson wearing a starched red-and-white checkered shirt under a pair of dark-blue denim bib overalls, a pair of red rubber boots on his feet. Instead of his cane, he gripped the handle of a brand-new shovel, the tip resting against the floor. A single white rose was pinned to one of the straps of his overalls.

"You're the gardener!" EJ immediately understood Mrs. Winkle's vision for the wedding. "Mrs. Winkle knew you didn't want to get dressed up in a tux, so she themed the wedding with things you love—gardening, flowers, and bluebirds!"

EJ covered her mouth with her hand, afraid she'd given away too much.

"You got it, EJ-girl!" Mrs. Winkle's voice came through the closed door. "Just wait till you see the auditorium!"

"What in all of creation do you have up your sleeve, Wilma?" Mr. Johnson nervously smoothed his parted and slicked hair with the palm of his hand.

"You'll see, sweetheart." EJ could tell that Mrs. Winkle loved having a secret surprise in store for the groom. "Just relax and enjoy the fact that you aren't wearing dress clothes."

"Mr. Johnson, Dad says it's time to start!" Isaac bounded down the hallway, dressed just like a mini version of Mr. Johnson except carrying a small silver bucket filled with potting soil, two ring boxes sitting on top.

"See you at the front of the church, Wilma," Mr. Johnson called. "I'll be the one with dirt under my fingernails."

EJ gave Mr. Johnson a thumbs-up before he walked toward the backstage door to meet Dad.

The excitement of the dress unveiling had boosted EJ's alertness for a few minutes, but as she walked with Mom, Faith, Isaac, and Bert to the doors of the auditorium, she felt her eyelids begin to droop again. She took a deep inhale of the fragrance coming off her flower bouquet of buttercups and white carnations and glanced down at Bert, who she held on a leash. He didn't seem thrilled with the ring of flowers around his neck, but at least he wasn't scratching at them anymore.

"You're gonna do great, Bertie," EJ said. "Everybody will be talking about how my dog is almost as smart and as talented as

I am." Bert gave a little sniff, indicating that he wasn't impressed with compliments like that. EJ smiled and patted his head.

EJ peeked into the auditorium to see that it had been transformed into something that looked like it came straight from the pages of the book *The Secret Garden*. The middle aisle was a lovely stone pathway with a rainbow of flowers lining the sides of the pews. The aisle led to a white picket fence on the stage, where even more flowers decorated the top of the fence. A white birdhouse stood on a pole on one side of the stage with two holes marked "His" and "Hers," and a small fountain stood on the other side of the stage—real water tumbling over smooth rocks and into a pool.

The small crowd of wedding guests was all seated, and most seemed mesmerized by the beauty around them. EJ recognized almost everyone sitting in the pews—mostly people from church along with Mrs. Winkle's bowling league and a few of Mr. Johnson's relatives—and she was glad to see Dane sitting in the front row, keeping her ukulele safe until she needed it to play and sing Mrs. Winkle down the aisle.

EJ watched as Dad, dressed in a dark brown suit, led the gardener-groom to their spot in front of the picket fence. She heard soft nature sounds come on over the speakers—birds singing, bees buzzing, and a soft breeze through the unseen trees—completing the wedding garden feeling.

"That's your cue, buddy," Mom said to Isaac. "Don't forget to lay the trail for Bert."

"On it." Isaac stuck his free hand in his pocket and confidently walked down the aisle. Every two steps, he dropped a dog treat from his pocket on the pathway. Bert strained against the leash, and EJ tightened her grip. "Not yet, Bert. Just one more minute."

When Isaac reached the front row of pews, he turned around and saluted at EJ, the secret sign he said he'd give when it was Bert's turn. "Okay, here we go." EJ nodded at Mom and unclipped the leash from Bert's collar. Bert bolted for the nearest treat and gobbled it up.

"Squeeeee!" Faith made a dash toward Bert, and Bert turned back with a twinkle in his eye. Tag had become one of his and Faith's favorite games since the first time she'd run after him and trapped him in the dryer. Once he knew she didn't *actually* want to hurt him, he was up for the fun. Bert and Faith made their way down the aisle, Bert from treat to treat, and Faith throwing handfuls of pink flower petals at the dog when she could get close enough to him, giggling and shrieking all the way down the aisle. Everyone in the auditorium laughed, and there were lots of flashes from cameras.

Mom was waiting with a bone for Bert and a bag of yogurt puffs for Faith at the front of the aisle when they got there, and she ushered them to a spot on the front pew. Once they were settled, eyes swiveled to the aisle, where EJ stood in the doorway.

"Love you, EJ-girl," Mrs. Winkle said behind her. "You'll do great."

EJ smiled at the beautiful bride. "I love you, too, Mrs. Winkle." She walked down the aisle, concentrating on smiling and not tripping over her own feet. She saw Mom turn around, point, and whisper to Faith, "There's your sister!" Faith's and Bert's little faces peeked over the back of the pew to watch her. EJ turned her head straight and saw Dad's smile and the giant grin that seemed to light up Mr. Johnson's whole face. Even Isaac was beaming at her. These were some of the people that she loved most in the world—people that she would do anything for, and she knew they would do anything for her. Suddenly she felt an overwhelming feeling of gratefulness.

As she arrived at the front pew, Dane handed her ukulele to her, took her flowers, and winked at her. "All tuned and ready to go, EJ."

"Thanks," she whispered and stepped up onto the stage. She paused for a moment to get the right finger placement on the instrument's frets and then began to strum the chord for the song's intro. . . .

And at that precise moment, her mind went blank.

Not just "give me the first word and I'll be able to go from there" blank but "what even is the name of the song I am supposed to play? And what is my name, for that matter?" blank. Sweat poured out of EJ's hands and forehead as she continued to strum the first chord over and over again. She felt her eyes unfocus as a wave of nerves overtook her, but she forced herself to look up and send a panicked look Dane's way, hoping her eyes said, "Please, help me!"

Dane calmly mouthed the next two chord names to EJ, and somehow her brain understood what he was saying. Her fingers knew what to do—thanks to the hours of practice she had put in on the song—and she continued strumming the introduction. She got to the end of the introduction and realized she still didn't remember any of the words to the song. *Sunbeam? Sunlight? Something with the sun?* All those eyes were staring at her—she had to do this! Come on, EJ!

The nature soundtrack playing over the sound system seemed

much louder as the final chord of the intro faded into silence. EJ stood frozen on the spot as someone in the pews cleared a throat nervously. EJ was ruining Mrs. Winkle's wedding. Her big moment—and she was blowing it!

"You are my sunshine, my only sunshine. . . ." Isaac's clear singing voice rang out, and EJ's fingers remembered the chords to the song that she had rehearsed countless times.

"You make me happy, when skies are gray," EJ started singing with Isaac, hoping that he'd keep singing, because she still didn't trust her exhausted brain to remember the words.

"You'll never know, dear, how much I love you." Mr. Johnson's deep voice joined in. EJ had never heard him sing before, so his fantastic voice caught her a little off guard.

"Please don't take my sunshine away." Mrs. Winkle's beautiful alto voice added to the voices as she walked toward the front of the auditorium. The next time through the simple chorus all of the wedding guests joined in, and EJ focused on playing the chords and enjoyed listening to the harmonies that some of the voices added. Mrs. Winkle took her spot next to Mr. Johnson at the end of the verse.

"I love a good sing-along," the bride whispered to EJ. "Well done, to both of you." She reached over and gave Isaac a pat on the head.

"Hey, Mr. Johnson, do you want the rings now?" Isaac's "whisper" was loud enough that the rest of the auditorium could clearly hear what he was saying. "I think the worms in this bucket are trying to eat the rings." Isaac pulled an earthworm from his pail. EJ gasped, horrified that Isaac could go from helpful and sweet to disgustingly boy in the span of thirty seconds, but she heard the chuckle from the stage spread through the audience.

"Worms are a hazard of the gardening occupation, Isaac," Mr. Johnson said. "We'll deal with the creepy crawlies when the ring part comes in a few minutes."

"Okay, but don't say I didn't warn you," Isaac said, poking the worm back in the dirt. "They look awful hungry."

Dad cleared his throat and started the ceremony.

"Friends and family, we are gathered here today to join Wilma and Lester together in holy matrimony. . . ."

EJ smiled, her heart full.

Dear Diary,

The rest of the wedding went perfectly.

(That's how this diary entry *should* start.)

But there were moments of insanity. Like when Isaac got bored during the vows and started swinging the pail by the handle and accidently showered the back of Mr. Johnson with the two wedding rings, three pounds of potting soil, and nine earthworms. (Isaac counted them when he and Mr. Johnson

picked them up in the middle of the ceremony.) Or when Bert got loose and made a game of weaving through wedding guests' ankles under the church pews. Although, I have to admit, it was pretty funny seeing the bowling league ladies jump up onto the seats and scream like they'd seen a mouse. Those women can move like they're *much* younger than they actually are!

But these things that might have ruined any other bride's special day seemed to actually make Mrs. Winkle all the happier. It's not just that she likes being creative and unconventional, it's that she genuinely loves people for who they are and she doesn't get nervous or upset when things don't go the way she thinks they should.

I'd like to be more like her (in more ways than one).

The wedding reception was a picnic in the park behind Mr. Johnson's house—and that part did pretty much go perfectly. We spread colorful quilts on the ground and on picnic tables and stuffed ourselves silly on Cady's catered food that was nowhere as fancy as the samples we tried at her shop a few weeks ago. Instead, Mrs. Winkle decided on fruit, pasta salad, potato salad, fresh-cut vegetables, and—Mr. Johnson got what he wanted—deli meat sandwiches (on crescent rolls to give them the proper amount of wedding classiness).

Mrs. Winkle hired Dane and his band to play music during the reception, and my favorite song was when he played the guitar, harmonica, and the kick drum at the same time. I always knew he could be a one-man band if he really wanted to.

Isaac got his chance to be the wedding comedian, and I have to admit that he has come a long way in his routine. In fact, he didn't even use his "Noah good joke" knock-knock joke! After he was done, I told him he did a good job, and you would've thought I had told the kid he'd just won a million dollars, he looked that pleased with himself.

Today was a good day. A best of days.

There have been so many changes for my family and friends in the past couple of years, Diary. From playing the angel in the nativity play and Code Christmas to church camp and finding out that Faith was going to join our family—real life is definitely an adventure! If I'm completely honest, Diary, Spooner, Wisconsin, is still too small and too much of a snooze-fest for my taste. But that doesn't mean that I don't love it here and love the people in my life. I guess when it comes down to it, I know that they need me and I need them. I don't know what the future holds, but I do know that we can get through it together.

And anyway, even in the boringest of places, one thing I know is that my imagination can take me anywhere I want to go!

EJ

Six months later...

"EJ, would you please go get Isaac and Faith? They're playing upstairs, I think." Mom stood in the kitchen, wearing oven mitts that made her hands look like lobster claws. "It's almost time to go for Thanksgiving dinner at Mrs. Winkle's house."

"I think you mean *Mr. and Mrs. Johnson's* house." EJ pulled a large wicker basket from the pantry and set it on the table. After Mrs. Winkle and Mr. Johnson got married, he and his cat, Gruff, moved into the house next to the Paynes. EJ was relieved because she liked Mrs. Winkle's house much better than Mr. Johnson's. Bert wasn't too thrilled that Gruff lived next door now—mostly because he was deathly afraid of cats.

"Oh! Right! *Mrs. Johnson* just doesn't quite roll off the tongue like *Mrs. Winkle* does." Mom opened the oven door and took out a dish of steaming green bean casserole that she placed in the basket. "It's hard to believe they've already been married for six months."

"Time flies when you're having fun, Tabby." Dad gave Mom a quick peck on the cheek in between putting together a big bowl of salad to take to the Thanksgiving meal. "Speaking of time, EJ, hurry and get the other two. I know you don't want to miss whatever culinary creativity Wilma has up her sleeve!"

EJ took the stairs two at a time, Bert at her heels, and the pair walked past the bathroom to the three kids' bedrooms.

"Okay, Faith, that's good. But I think you can do better." Isaac's voice drifted through the six-inch gap of Faith's bedroom door that was mostly shut. Whatever he was telling his little sister sounded serious. EJ tiptoed toward the door to peek in, unnoticed. What she saw made her smile: Faith sat on the floor while Isaac paced in front of her, hands clasped behind his back. The two were surrounded by Isaac's dinosaur collection—stuffed dinos, action-figure dinos with moving heads, legs, and tails, rubberized fossil dino skeletons, and even a remote-controlled brontosaurus that always seemed a little creepy to EJ. Faith happily clutched Isaac's favorite T-Rex toy that was dressed up with several flower headbands around the dinosaur's neck, belly, and tail. The eighteen-month-old's bright eyes watched Isaac's every move.

Bert gave a little huff next to EJ as the two peered through the crack. "Better that T-Rex than you, buddy," EJ whispered to her pooch.

"Now this is the most important part, Faith." Isaac stopped pacing and sat on the floor, facing his little sister. "This is the part where you really hit a home run or you strike out."

"Ho-run," Faith repeated.

"Yes, that's what we want—a home run." Isaac took the T-Rex from Faith and set it aside. "So I say, 'Noah who?' and *you* say. . . ?" Isaac looked expectantly at her.

Faith flashed her tiny baby teeth at Isaac in the cutest smile on the face of the earth.

"Yes! That's good, Faith! If there's one thing I've learned, being adorable will get you out of lots of trouble!" Isaac got serious. "But we've got to finish this. I say, 'Noah who?'. . ."

Faith scrunched her face and thought hard. Then she took a deep breath and shouted, "No-uh good jote?"

EJ had to cover her mouth to keep a laugh from escaping. Faith's delivery of the punch line of Isaac's joke was funnier than anytime she'd heard Isaac tell it.

"Excellent job, Faith!" Isaac lifted his hand, and she slapped her chubby palm against his in a high-five. "That knock-knock joke has served me well. And now it's time to pass it on. Use it wisely, young Jedi."

EJ's stomach growled, reminding her it was time for Thanksgiving dinner. She didn't want her brother and sister to know she'd been spying on them, so she turned her face away from the doorway and threw her voice toward the top of the stairs so it didn't sound like she was right outside Faith's bedroom door. "Faith! Isaac! Mom says it's time to leave!"

"Coming!" Isaac called and then turned his attention back to Faith. "Another thing I need to teach you is how to annoy EJ. It's so much fun." EJ strained to hear as Isaac dropped his voice to a whisper. "*I'm* the Space Invader, but if you figure out new ways to bug her, she might give you a super-cool nickname, too. EJ is awesome like that."

EJ opened the door and stuck her head inside, breaking up the brain trust of little siblings. "Ready to go, Space Invader? What about you, Miss Messy?"

"Messy!" Faith scooped up an armload of stuffed animals and chucked them across the room to illustrate her new nickname. Faith giggled, grabbed EJ's hand, and gazed happily up at her big sister.

"Let's go!" Isaac led his sisters through the doorway and bounded toward the steps. "Faith's got a joke that everybody's gonna love!"

About the Author

Annie Tipton made up her first story at the ripe old age of two when she asked her mom to write it down for her. (Hey, she was just two—she didn't know how to make letters yet!) Since then she has read and written many words as a student, newspaper reporter, author, and editor. Annie loves snow (which is a good thing because she lives in Ohio), wearing scarves, sushi, Scrabble, and spending time with friends and family.

Book 1: True Story

Will EJ become part of the adventure of the real Christmas story—and discover that her *little* role in the Christmas pageant in *little* old Spooner, Wisconsin, really isn't so *little* at all?

Available Now!

Book 2: Church Camp Chaos

It's *Church Camp Chaos*—complete with bunk beds, campfires, and s'mores—for lovable EJ in this second fantastic release in the Diary of a Real Payne series.

Available Now!